drinks at minks

A RUBY'S COMPANION NOVELLA

DL WHITE

BOOKS

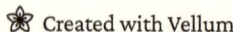

drinks at minks

author's note

Return to the booth where it all began.

Ten years after they first captured readers' hearts, Renee, Maxine, and Debra are back, navigating new chapters of life with the same honesty, humor, and deep friendship that made their story unforgettable.

Renee Gladwell finally has the bookstore running smoothly, but her father's worsening Alzheimer's has her confronting mortality and legacy in ways she never expected. When her rock-solid boyfriend Malcolm receives an unexpected call from his ex-wife, Renee must face what she truly wants for her future.

Maxine Donovan built her luxury real estate empire through determination and independence. Now, with a family, she's planning an ambitious expansion, but as Joseph's career takes off too, their competing ambitions threaten the delicate balance they've created.

Debra Macklin has rebuilt her life since the scandal that nearly cost her everything. When an unexpected opportunity for advancement presents itself, she must decide if she's ready to step back into leadership – and if her healing marriage can withstand the pressure.

As life pulls them in different directions, their standing Saturday brunch at Ruby's becomes harder to maintain. But when challenges arise, these three women know exactly where to turn...to the friendship that has sustained them through every triumph and heartbreak.

Warm, witty, and deeply emotional, this epilogue to the beloved *Brunch at Ruby's* novel delivers the perfect blend of new beginnings and satisfying closure for readers who have waited to revisit their favorite fictional friends.

Author's Note: This epilogue continues the journey of characters from the original Brunch at Ruby's. For the fullest experience, readers are encouraged to enjoy the original story first.

Drinks at Minks continues the journey of three friends navigating life's complexities with honesty and heart. While their stories contain moments of joy and triumph, they also reflect real-life challenges that may resonate deeply with some readers. Please be advised of the following content advisories:

• References to infidelity and extramarital affairs
• Depiction of dementia and cognitive decline in an elderly parent
• Discussion of divorce and its emotional aftermath
• Marital conflict and relationship struggles
• References to grief and loss (including deceased family members)
• Mild sexual content (implied intimate scenes)
• Discussions about marriage and family planning

one

RENEE

I pace the kitchen, phone pressed to my ear. Above my head, footsteps thump across the floor, then thunder down the stairs through the living room. Malcolm rounds the corner, his phone in one hand, the soft leather case he's had forever in the other.

"Hi, good morning," I say, as the line connects. "Could I get Bernard Gladwell's room, please?"

"Talking to your dad?" Malcolm whispers, gathering his keys, wallet, badge.

"Waiting for them to connect me."

"I've gotta run. Brent has an early meeting I need to attend."

I tilt my face up, savoring the quick kiss he lays on my lips. "Love you, have a good day, take your— Hi, Daddy!" My father's voice, thin as tissue paper, interrupts my goodbye. I point at the brown paper lunch bag I packed, making sure

1

Malcolm grabs it before he disappears into the garage with a wave.

"Who's this?" He asks.

"It's Renee, Daddy."

"Renee?"

"Noodle," I prod, using the nickname that sometimes unlocks his memory. "Your daughter?"

"Oh. Alright..."

"How you doing today, Daddy? Did you have breakfast?"

"Uh...yes. I had breakfast."

"Good. Did you eat it all?"

"Yeah."

"Did you go for your walk?"

"Yeah."

"Okay, good." I pause, waiting for him to say more, but lately, he's more reactive than initiator. His language slipping away. "Okay Daddy. I just wanted to talk to you. You have therapy today."

"Therapy. Yes."

"Don't give those nice people any problems. Did you see Jessie today?"

"Jessie?"

"The big nurse, Daddy. She works at Golden Rays now."

"Babysitter."

I chuckle. "Yes Daddy. The babysitter. Did you see her?"

"Uh huh... what's your name?"

"Renee, Daddy. My name is Renee."

Every morning, I call Daddy in his room at Golden Rays. I catch him early, while his mind is fresh, before the confusion of afternoon sets in and he starts to sundown—forgetting things, people, places, himself. He's only been at Golden Rays a few months, but he's adjusting so well.

I worried about moving him, feared watching the memories of his home with Lorraine fade faster, watching him forget the daughter whose name he already struggles to recall.

That forgetting doesn't cut as deeply anymore. This Bernard Gladwell doesn't forget my name out of spite or anger. He simply can't remember. And I can't hold on to hurt about something he can't control.

Despite everything we tried, keeping him at home became impossible. Even with Jessie living with us and Malcolm helping, Daddy needed more therapy, other people, specialized care I couldn't provide. I was so busy managing his condition that I couldn't just be his daughter anymore. A year after Jessie moved in to care for him, Malcolm and I sat down with her, and together we made the decision to move him to the Memory Care Center at Golden Rays.

The blessing was that Dr. Ron hired Jessie immediately. Daddy still sees her every day, and her job comes with housing. She's found her purpose caring for the memory care patients, and I found space to breathe.

That left Malcolm and me alone in our house. Some days I feel like we've become that couple who've already raised their kids and sent them into the world, now just looking at each other in an empty house and rediscovering who we are together.

I stay on the phone with Daddy until it's time for his therapy. They play memory games, exercise daily, and track his Alzheimer's with monthly evaluations. Surprisingly, he's stable; even doing better in some ways than when he first arrived.

After saying goodbye, I scroll through my favorites and call Maxine. She and Joseph live just blocks away, and I know she's already up, probably halfway through her morning routine.

"Why are you calling me at this time of morning, Renee?"

Maxine snaps, by way of greeting. "What if I was in bed with my husband, giving him some of that Good Maxine?"

"Because I know you're awake and your Good Maxine blocker would never let morning sex happen."

Maxine sucks her teeth, then laughs. "It's a shame how right you are." She sighs, but it's one of those content, happy sighs. I've learned to tell the difference between that and a *someone-come-get-this-baby* sigh. "You talked to Bernard already?"

"Yeah, I talked to him. Malcolm just left for work. You sound tired."

"You know when you were taking care of your dad, how I used to tell you all the time that you sounded tired and you were grumpy?"

"Mmmmm..."

"Well, now I get it. I've never been so exhausted in my life."

I'm loving seeing Maxine get her ass handed to her after so many years of looking down her nose at other people. "How many times last night?"

"Up every two hours like clockwork. And she wouldn't take the bottle for Joseph so I was up every two hours." Maxine yawns an unladylike roar. "Inell says she's spoiled. And of course, now that I need to take her over there, she's fast asleep and I don't want to wake her up."

I chuckle, though under my breath.

"I hear you laughing over there. You wait until you pop out a little one. What do you want, Renee?"

"I was going to come by for coffee if you were up for it. Or I could run by the coffeeshop and grab us something."

"You know what I like."

I do know her order by heart, so I slip my bag over my shoulder and head out to the car for a short trip to the neighborhood coffee shop, then to Max and Joseph's and a visit with my niece, Imani. She's perfect—dark, curly hair, bright brown eyes, the roundest cheeks you ever saw on a baby, and pudgy little limbs. She's a plump and happy dollop...when she's not hungry. Or wet. Or tired. Or bothered in general.

When I was younger, and I did things my mother didn't understand, she'd tell me that she hoped I didn't have children like me. Well, no one told Maxine that. Imani is so much like her mother, it's frightening.

Maxine meets me at the door with the baby perched on one arm. They're both wearing a luscious pink and I'm betting even Imani wears a designer label.

"There's my little doo wop chocolate drop!" I coo at her with the usual fanfare and custom nickname. She gives me a gummy smile, then a throaty gurgle of laughter.

Maxine takes the venti double espresso mocha that I picked up for her and lets me take the baby. I bounce her gently and revel in the sweet scent of baby shampoo in my nostrils, fat little hands gripping my shirt and sweet sounds coming from her mouth.

Before meeting Malcolm and seeing Maxine with a baby, I'd never seriously considered having children. I'd missed most of Debra's pregnancy and a lot of Kendra's growing up. And with Marcus, the idea of children never crossed my mind. But now...things are different. I'm older, wiser, settled. Malcolm and I are more solid than I'd ever imagined we'd be, and thoughts of taking another huge leap with him have been running rampant through my mind.

"You must be headed into the office. Busy day in real estate?"

Maxine sips hot coffee as quickly as she can.

"The market right now is so aggressive. I can't keep inventory current, they're selling so fast. We're busting at the seams; I need to hire more agents and since Imani was born I haven't been able to work back up to full time." She drops onto the white leather Natuzzi couch she has had for years.

I still can't believe she sold her Buckhead Atlanta condo, but after she and Joseph moved into the house, there wasn't a need to hang onto it. With upgrades to the property and improvements in the market, she made a killing on the sale.

I lower myself to the couch a few cushions away from her and try to drink my latte without the baby knocking it from my hands. I manage a sip or two and then set the cup on the coffee table in front of me.

"Isn't it Virgil's job to worry about that stuff?" Her long-suffering assistant and General Manager is a real estate machine. He's also snooty and pretentious and treats me like belly button lint whenever I happen to talk to him. Although, I've been reassured, he treats everyone that way.

"He's already working ten-hour days, trying to fill in for me. I need to get back to one hundred percent. I don't know how Debra does this working and raising children thing."

The third Musketeer to our gang of childhood friends, Debra, is the Suzy Homemaker of the group, the one who has it all, knows it all, always has an answer. These days, she's been concentrating on rebuilding her life.

"I don't think Debra did it very well. That's how she ended up losing her job."

"She didn't lose her job, Renee. She resigned."

"After they offered her a Sabbatical in lieu of firing her."

"She voluntarily left."

I roll my eyes but smile inwardly. Maxine and Debra pick at each other like sisters, but no one can pick at Debra except Maxine. Not even me.

"Have you seen Debra lately? Since she took that Assistant Director's position at the Community Center, all I get is hi and bye from her."

I shake my head. "Not in a while. We have lunch plans at Ruby's today, though. Want to join us?"

Max frowns. "Thanks for thinking of me, best friends. I can't go anyway; I have to drop Imani at Inell's and get to the office. Virgil has already called me three times today."

Imani kicks her little legs and whines, her arms outstretched for Maxine. Out of instinct, Max reaches for her and gathers the baby to her chest, plopping a trail of kisses across her cheek. "I guess we'd better get ready, so Grandma can get busy spoiling you."

I stand, helping Max gather the diaper bag and her purse and follow her to the car. She straps Imani into her seat and drops another kiss on a pudgy cheek before backing out and closing the door. It's still strange to see an infant carrier in the back of the pristine white Maserati—a car that now, according to Joseph, occasionally sports smashed cheerios and milk stains.

"You know," she huffs, catching her breath from all of that activity, "we haven't had brunch in forever. Debra works every other weekend, you and Malcolm have your... well, I don't even know what y'all are doing over there, with the yard and everything. And my weekends are so full. Maybe we need to switch some things up, because a group text is just not going to cut it for me. I miss my girls. And I'm tired of missing my girls."

"I know. It seems like things have changed so much—"

"Because they have. I'll put some thought into it. Maybe we have drinks one night instead."

"There's an idea. Drop it into the group chat so we can all talk about it."

Max pulls at the crisp peplum at her waist. "Well, off I go. I'm every woman, and all that Oprah feel good shit."

We laugh as I hug her, then I step back and let her get into the car before I head to my own car. Smiling, sipping coffee, singing along to the radio, I am bound for Lorraine Gladwell Books.

A few years ago, Daddy's decline brought the bookstore to near collapse. It was a struggle to bring the business back to life, especially when my goal was to sell it. Lately, the place is bustling. We've done some rearranging and redecorating, adding more books by authors that my mother would have loved. Betty's Coffee & Smoothies pays consistent rent, the study rooms Malcolm built last summer stay booked, and the bistro tables with colorful umbrellas draw the university crowd to our sidewalk. Gladwell Books feels alive again.

My manager, Lexie, always has some grand idea for an event or a way to use the space. Her energy is adorable and contagious. I let her have run of the shop and the staff while I take care of the finances and work on future business ideas. Malcolm thinks we should add a second level to the building, but that's not the kind of expanding I've been thinking about lately.

I push away these thoughts as I pull into my spot behind the bookstore. I've arrived later than usual, so the parking lot is already dotted with cars. I enter the shop through the back-door, greeted by the sounds of commerce—the whir of Betty's smoothie blender, the click of register keys, faint conversation in the book stacks.

I head to my office and unload my bag and my coffee, boot up the computer and login.

"Oh, you're here!"

I glance up to find Lexie standing in the doorway of my office. She's always worn her hair in an intricate tangle of micro-braids. They frame her face and make her look much younger than her twenty-eight years. She's the proud holder of an MFA, and I'd been worried that she'd be looking to move on from Gladwell, but she seems as rooted as ever to the bookstore and keeping the business alive.

She talked me into hiring a part time social media manager and capitalizing on being one of the few Black woman owned bookshops in our area, let alone in the city. I have to admit she was right to insist—online orders have been booming and foot traffic has increased measurably. Mama would be so proud of her little bookshop.

"Yeah. I had a long talk with Daddy, then I stopped over to see Maxine and the baby. How's business this morning?"

"The usual."

I wave her in and Lexie steps over the threshold into my office and settles into the chair in front of my desk, tucking one leg under the other. This office used to be my mother's; this desk and this chair were hers. I love the idea of sitting in the same spot where she sat and talked with me when I clerked for her after school.

"Did you need me for something? I wanted to finish going through these invoices before lunch."

"Oh, not really. I just had a thought about something and wondered... well, it's about my son."

Lexie's son is the cutest sci-fi fan you ever met.

"He's here a couple of nights a week, waiting for me to get off but he's been so bored. I was thinking... what if we put together young adult book club? Something for the kids to do after school, that encourages reading and socializing?"

My eyebrows lift in curiosity and deep thought. Debra buys books for her community center reading program, but I'd never thought about hosting the kids here.

"That's not a bad idea. Gladwell could offer the books at a discount for members and maybe Betty would provide healthy snacks?"

Lexie grins, leaning forward and settling her elbows on my

desk. "That's what I was thinking! But really let the kids design their own book club. Let them read whatever books they want to read, then let them get together and discuss them. I think it would do so much for critical thinking and encourage them to read past whatever popular author is out today."

I lean back, swiveling the chair one way and then the other. "Do you have time to manage it?"

Her head bobs vigorously.

I shrug my shoulders. "Run anything you need to use petty cash for by me, as usual. Use the staff if you need them and let me know if I can help with anything. Okay?"

Satisfied, she stands and heads toward the door. "Thanks. I think this is going to be a great idea. I'll talk to Leo about what he'd like to do and let him help me put it together."

"The kids will love it. Thanks, Lex," I call out, but she's already gone back to work in the shop.

I try to focus on my work, but I'm interrupted by a text from Debra:

> Are we still meeting for lunch?

> Yep. And I'll bring your books. I need to drop by the bank first. If you get there before me, get a table.

> Okay. See you in a bit!

two

DEBRA

I grab the box of "Tristan Strong Punches a Hole in the Sky" that I ordered from Renee and trek from the car to my office at East Lake Community Center. The new job was a blessing in disguise. It sparked real interest in community education and put me back in touch with the students, the whole reason I went into education.

And it pulled me out of the politics of public schools and away from Charlotte Rogers.

I heard she left the PTA, but as long as she has eyes and ears around that school, tongues will wag, people will keep the scandal alive, and my mistakes will affect Kendra. So we pulled her from Morningside and enrolled her at Tucker Preparatory, a private school in our district.

Kendra has taken a keen interest in math and science, and Willard and I wanted to push her in that direction. She threw a fit at first about not being able to see her friends, but she soon realized that they all live around us and she can still see them after school and on weekends.

Besides, a boy she likes goes to Tucker. She is too excited to go to school every day. I may not survive high school.

When I had my accident and subsequent reckless driving charge, part of my restitution was volunteering at a community center. I fell in love with the atmosphere, with the kids, with the youthful, invigorating tempo. I had forgotten what it was like to work one-on-one with the kids, to impact them directly, not through dress code policies and senseless, district-wide mandates that didn't benefit anyone but administration. And I've loved not having to conduct testing over the last year.

So I didn't go back to Gwinnett. When my sabbatical was over, I tendered my resignation and began working full-time as Assistant Director of Youth Programs at East Lake. The pay cut was painful. Losing my status as Principal at Morningside, a job I'd worked so hard to attain, was painful.

I don't regret it. I needed a change, and it saved my marriage.

Now I pop into my office around 9AM, check the mail and email, then make my rounds to the activity rooms in the two-story facility. We run a number of education and social programs, from before and after school care to GED classes, to tutoring services and study sessions. We also have activity rooms and a full gym for intramural sports. I manage the staff and I teach when needed, but my heart is the reading program.

We switch themes regularly and we read a book a month. When I first started the program, I had just a few participants; now the program is fifty kids strong and growing.

I drop the books off at the Reading Room, a spacious area painted in bright colors, furnished with plush couches and bean bag chairs. The kids come in twice a week for an activity that we call Drop Every Thing and Read. They grab a book, settle in, and read for a specific amount of time. When they're finished, they check the books back in and move on to another activity. We're amassing such a great library of used books, sometimes I find parents in the room waiting for their child to finish a game or tutoring session.

I'm almost bowled over by Camille, one of our Activities Directors, as I leave the reading room. Her full figure is draped in a thick cream cable knit sweater and chocolate brown leggings. The heels of her knee-high boots pound against the linoleum.

"Oh hey!" I laugh and duck out of her way. She seems hell-bent on getting somewhere yesterday. "Where are you headed?"

"After-school room. We have a situation."

"Whoa, wait a minute." I grab her by the elbow, nearly dislodging an armful of art supplies—butcher paper, glue sticks, stamps, stickers, even some glitter. "What kind of situation, Cam?"

She blows a wavy strand of hair out of her face and readjusts the pile in her arms. "Mariah called out. Again. At the last minute. Again." She gives me a look.

I return it with one that tells her not to waste her time complaining. I'm doing what I can to help Mariah without firing her, but I'm at my wit's end, too.

"I had to find someone to take over my room so I could fill in for her. Kids are about to show up in..." A glance at her watch sends her eyebrows up to her hairline. "A few minutes. I grabbed what I could get my hands on and I'm heading to the room now. Most of the kids will settle in with homework, but you know some of them need to be occupied."

"Do you need me to come help?"

She shakes her head. Camille is so blessedly self-sufficient. "But Ms. Henry was looking for you a few minutes ago."

"Okay. Well, watch your ratios and grab someone if you need help. I'll be here until five."

Camille turns to continue her march down the hall. "Okay, Ms. Debra! Thank you!"

The mention of Ms. Henry's name strikes fear in the hearts of some. She's a stodgy, stern, all-business woman with a take-no-prisoners attitude, but I also know her to be fair and, at rare times, kind and understanding. She knew my history before she offered me the job at ELCC and let me prove myself to her. Besides, I've been in her shoes and I know what it's like to always have to play the bad guy.

Her office door is slightly open, the sound of her acrylic nails clicking on the keyboard wafting through the crack.

"Knock, knock." I gently push the door open and stick my head inside.

Eleanor's office is orderly, all of her work in neat stacks, her phone at one hand, her computer at the other. Only when she finishes the sentence she's typing does she lift her head to greet me.

"Debra, come in." She pushes away from her desk, pulling a pair of bifocals from her eyes. They hang on a chain around her neck and come to rest on her ample bosom as she sits back in her chair.

I step inside and take a seat. "Everything okay? There aren't any complaints or problems, are there?"

"Nothing like that. I wanted to discuss something with you."

I shift in my seat, then cross one leg over the other. "Sounds serious."

"It's not all that serious. In fact, it's rather joyous. The thing is, Debra..." She bows her head and presses her thin lips together. She wears a gaudy shade of red lipstick every single day. No one dares tell Ms. Henry that NARS Red Lizard doesn't go well with her yellow undertones.

After a few beats, she lifts her face and fixes her gaze to mine. "I'm going to be retiring at the end of this year." She blinks, then gives me a solitary nod.

"Oh... wow," I respond, finding my voice. "Retiring. How long have you been here? Thirty years?"

She chuckles, then scoots her chair in and leans her forearms on the desk. The expression on her face is one of wistful nostalgia. "Thirty-five if you count the years I volunteered before they could pay me. When I started, ELCC was a one-story building. We had about three rooms, nothing outdoors but some grass. Real low-rent kind of place. We didn't add the second level until about... oh, twenty years ago, with the intention to expand further."

"You sure have ushered this place through some change, Ms. Henry. I'm surprised, to say the least. I can't imagine ELCC without you here."

"Debra...they're about to post for my position. I want you to apply."

She keeps talking, despite the fact that my jaw is nearly resting on my chest.

"In fact, I insist on it. I'll champion you through the process with the City Council member that stewards our relationship with the city. You've met Dr. West, haven't you?"

I manage a slight dip of my chin. I knew Dr. West in my former life as a middle school principal.

"You have more than sufficient experience, and you've done a fine job with the place since you came on. I think you'd fill my shoes well."

"I... I... I don't know what to say. I'm honestly speechless, Eleanor."

She reaches for her glasses and slips them onto the bridge

of her nose. "You'd better think of some things to say, and quickly. Start reviewing yourself and your performance here. Mine, too. What would you have done differently? What will you keep the same? How would you usher ELCC into a new age while keeping the tenets and mission intact? All of these things are going to be important to the Board and Dr. West."

"But I—"

She waves a hand in the air, brushing away my protests. "I'm not trying to hear excuses, Debra. It'll be you or a venture capitalist or heaven forbid, some uptight accountant type—"

"I'm married to one of those, thank you."

"Would you want him to come into this office, straight from the outside with no knowledge of these kids and this neighborhood and this community and what it needs, trying to run this place based on a budget? Do you know how long I had to fight for something as simple as the Summer Smoothie Bar? The lines are out the door when it's open and Dr. West still won't admit it was a good idea."

She grunts, her vivid green eyes floating above the bifocal lenses, her cheeks magnified in the bottom halves of them.

"This center needs you, Debra. And you need it. Look how much you've grown since you came here. How much change you've brought to the atmosphere here. These kids need you at the top."

The words she speaks are so true, it scares me. ELCC has been my healing place. It's reminded me of what I love about our educational system. It's also shown me where it's faltered and where there's still work that needs to be done.

"I'm not making excuses or trying to argue at all, but...do you think Dr. West would consider me? He must already have someone in mind if you're trying to shoehorn me in early."

She begins to smile but then hides it away. "I've known Theodore West for a long time. If I don't tell him what he thinks, he'll try to form an opinion of his own. We don't want that."

My bottom lip creeps between my teeth. Outside in the hallway, sounds of the shuffle of feet and pre-adolescent voices ring out.

"We'll talk later, and I'm not taking no for an answer. Have I made myself clear?"

Solemn, I push the chair back and stand. "As a bell."

My drive home is mostly a daze, the coupe winding through the streets on automatic pilot. I'm contemplating the offer.

Taking over as Senior Director at ELCC would be an easy move, sure. It'd be like Morningside, but on a much smaller scale, with a much smaller budget. I'd have a staff that actually likes me and respects my position. I'd be serving children, parents, and a community that sorely needs ELCC, and I'd still be doing work that makes me feel good when I go home at night.

Another factor gives me a long, pregnant pause.

My face has been on the news, my name in the newspapers, my situation whispered in conversations from here to the next county over and beyond. I can't go to the grocery store without feeling like I'm on display, like I'm being talked about behind my back.

That's that woman who had the affair, then got drunk and almost killed herself.

I used to be entirely more active in professional organizations, even our HOA. I'm not saying I'd let some gossip keep me from an opportunity that I want to take advantage of. But I still have Kendra and Willard to think about. I wouldn't want to embarrass them, and my goal in the past year has been to put said scandal behind us.

Still, I'm giving the offer a second and third thought.

I turn into the driveway, smiling by habit at the blooming buds planted along both sides of the porch steps. The old swing Willard and I hung when we moved in hangs motion-less, painting an almost Rockwellian scene. I remember a time when that scene was so much a lie.

While things are the best I could ask for between us, Willard and I still have our issues. We still see a marriage coun-selor, though it's more monthly maintenance than weekly rebuilding. We still make the effort to stay on the right track. It's hard work, but I've loved that man since before I knew what love really was, and I'm not giving him up without a fight.

The house is warm and brightly lit when I come in through the garage. Kendra, still in her uniform of dark blue skirt and crisp white blouse, is seated at the kitchen table, earbuds in her ear, notebook, pen, and textbook in front of her. As always, her music is loud enough to hear across the room.

I pass her, tapping her on the shoulder as I do. Her head pops up and she pulls an earbud from her ear. "Hi Ma! I didn't hear you come in."

I snicker, dropping my bag to the table across from her and shrugging my jacket from my shoulders. I hang it on the back of a chair and push the sleeves of my sweater up over my elbows.

"It's a wonder you can hear anything. Do you have to listen to music that loud?"

She smiles, her braces making her grin glisten in the over-head lights. "It helps me concentrate. It blocks out all the other sounds and it's like it's so loud I can't hear it, you know?"

"That doesn't make any sense, Kendra. Turn it down some, 'kay?"

I open the refrigerator and pull out a package of chicken

breasts I'd taken out to defrost that morning. Unfortunately, they're still hard as a rock.

"Ugh. The chicken didn't defrost."

"Ooh, can we order pizza?" Her face brightens, even when I scowl in her direction.

Then I give up, knowing she would fight to the death for pizza. We don't order in often, but once in a while can't hurt.

"Get out the menu. I'm going to say hi to Daddy."

Just past the family room with the enormous TV that Kendra and I gave Willard about five Father's Days ago, past the formal living room that we almost never use, is the office at the front of the house. I hear the squeak of his favorite chair with the yellow stuffing seeping out of every hole. Willard has been talking about remodeling the office to give him more room to work. I'm looking forward to getting rid of that raggedy chair.

"I understand where you're coming from, Barry." The door to the office is cracked slightly. Willard's voice comes through loud and clear. I linger in the hallway, half listening but mostly waiting so I don't disturb him.

"I'm not doing any less work than anyone else in my division. In fact, I'm doing more because I can concentrate better at home. Me being up for partner should be about more than time in the office."

He groans, sucking his teeth as he does.

"Face time is a corporate consultant buzzword and you know it, Barry. If senior management thinks I'm not worthy of being a partner because I'm not up there all day every day, kissing ass and *yes sir, no sir, I made you so much money, sir,*' then maybe I don't need to be partner. I make the firm a lot of money, but maybe I don't need to be at Willoughby at all."

My jaw clenches at what I hear of the conversation. Willard has never hinted toward any problems he's having at the accounting firm. Willoughby is prestigious; his job is one that accountants covet. And if he wanted to just be a mid-level worker his whole life, it'd be a well-respected firm from which to retire.

But I know Willard. He has aspirations above being an Accountant and CPA. He moved a lot of his work home two years ago. I've loved having him around more, even if he's in his office most of the time. Lunch with my husband on a Saturday is as easy as walking to his office. Dinner with him at home every night has been wonderful, and just having him here around us has worked miracles for our marriage. We like each other again. Not just love each other but genuinely enjoy spending time together.

I feel guilty for listening to Willard's call, so I tiptoe back to the kitchen. Kendra is poring over the menu to our favorite pizza spot.

"Daddy is busy, but we know what he likes. What are we having?"

Kendra's brows are furrowed, scanning the menu. "How do you make a pizza low fat?"

"Low fat?" I stare at her like some kind of alien pod has replaced my daughter. "I can't believe I'm saying this, but it's pizza. If you want low fat, grab one of those gluten-free, card-board-tasting frozen things you hate out of the freezer."

"Maaaaa," she moans, but she's laughing, toying at the edges of the menu. "I don't want to get fat."

My eyes skip down her lithe figure—thin legs in dark tights, knee-length uniform skirt, medium blouse. She's tall and thin, but in weight range for her height.

"Who's got you worried about getting fat?"

"Calandra and some of the other sophomore girls were saying this one other girl was fat and that's why boys don't like her and that this other girl was cute but she didn't make the cheerleading squad 'cause she had a fupa—"

"Excuse me?" I choke out.

"It means a fat upper—"

"I know what it means, Kendra," I sputter, trying to recover. "Don't... don't say that word. You should stay away from those girls. If they're judging other girls like that, they're ugly on the inside. I don't want you picking that up."

"But they're my friends—"

My eyebrows shoot up involuntarily as I stare at my daughter. "Are they? If they talk mess about other girls, are these the kids you want to be around? And you let them talk mess about other girls in front of you? What happens when they start talking about you?"

Kendra doesn't answer, but her eyelids lower and her lips poke out in a pout.

"I will not have you looking at yourself like those girls look at other girls. Because, my love..." I reach toward her, cup her chin in my palm and lift so I can see her bright brown eyes. "You are a beautiful, healthy, perfectly formed person. And I'm always right, so don't let anyone tell you different."

Kendra sucks her teeth and rolls her eyes, but I feel her skin warm. If she could blush, she would. "You're supposed to think that."

"Good, because I do. And I want you to think that, too. Mkay?"

She pauses for a beat, then nods. I release her and sit in the chair next to her. "So let's pick a pizza to share. How about the chicken and spinach we tried last time?"

three

MAXINE

Virgil is remarkably casual as I pass his desk. His feet are propped up on the corner, clad in a pair of brand-new Prada slippers. He's rifling through a thick stack of listings, which he tosses down when he sees me. The thunk of pages hitting his desk cuts through the quiet hum of the office.

"You will not believe how busy this day has been," he calls after me as I enter my office. "This is the first chance I've had to take a breath."

"It's only ten am, Virgil," I say, laughing a little. He has a flair for the dramatic that I find amusing. "How can it already be that busy?"

"I've been here since seven," he argues.

I try not to take it as a dig. I've always walked to the beat of my own drum, but Virgil used to hound me to show up to the office on time, especially for meetings. After Imani was born, it became obvious that I was never going to arrive before eight am ever again, so he gave up. The slight arch of his eyebrow tells me he hasn't completely forgotten, though.

"Maybe it's a full moon," I offer, settling in at my desk.

I hear him scoot his chair back and kick his legs down. Seconds later, he appears at my door. "Ready for messages?"

I groan. This is my least favorite part of the day and he knows it. The stack of pink slips in his hand seems thicker than usual. "Hit me with the highlights."

He drops into a chair and flips through slips of pink While You Were Out pages. "Sell me a house, sell me a house, I want to sell my house, blah blah blah. I've passed those along to the agents."

He flips through more slips of paper. "Hmmm... oh! You've been invited to sit on the Board of Directors for the Atlanta District of the Association of Women Realtors. They're sending a formal invite in the mail."

"Hooray," I respond dryly.

Another notch in my professional belt. Another organization wishing to use the Donovan name to further itself, push itself higher and claim to care about women owned business. Black women owned business, specifically. The recognition should feel good, but lately these accolades feel more like obligations than honors, and more like checking a box for the association than for me.

"You don't sound excited. They're the largest female run real estate organization in the country."

"I know that," I snap. "It's not that I'm not honored. I am. It's just..."

I shrug, my eye naturally drawn to the set of silver frames on the corner of my desk. One holds our first family portrait, taken just after Imani was born. The other is a candid shot of my baby girl sitting in the grass on a gorgeous day in a big, beautiful dress that Inell bought for her. The sunlight in the photo catches the deep brown of Imani's eyes, so much like Joseph's.

I still love running my own business; Donovan is my heart and soul. It bears my name. It's a part of me. But there's another part of me that I don't want to be away from one more minute than necessary.

"I understand," says Virgil. "Okay, I don't, really, not having had any children. I know you don't want to be away from your child or your husband. But I did inquire about the requirements to be on the board and they aren't that bad. Aside from the revenue and community involvement clauses, the meetings are only held quarterly, so there are only four a year, with child care available. They're all women, of course. You could take Imani with you to a board meeting."

He pauses, making sure I look up to catch his eye. His usual sharp gaze has softened. "Something to consider. It'd be a great move for you, especially if you're interested in this next message I'm about to relay."

The tone in Virgil's voice makes the hair on my neck stand up. It's usually a harbinger of something exciting. A challenge. Something new. That's exactly what I need. Anticipation flows through me, momentarily pushing aside thoughts of home and hearth.

"What are you talking about, Virgil?"

Smug, he lays the stack of pink squares on the desk and leans forward. His tone is low, conspiratorial. "How do we feel about commercial real estate?"

"Commercial Real Estate," I repeat. Curious, but my excitement is honestly waning. If I wanted to sell commercial properties, I would. "Like... not luxury homes?"

"Still luxury. Just not homes."

"Did you forget where you work, Virgil?"

He laughs quietly while offering me a small, condescending smile. That's a jovial as Virgil gets without a few shots of whiskey or a glass of merlot.

"I know exactly where I work. And I want to know if you're ready to move into the big time. Imagine, Maxine. Prime office space for the next political bigwig on the rise. Retail space for a rich Italian upscale eyewear designer—you know they control all the major eyewear outlets. We could be talking multiple locations. Instead of renting prefabricated cookie cutter mall space, we provide the finest of luxury commercial to call their own. They make money off of their investment. And so do we."

My head is spinning so fast with ideas that I'm unable to form a complete, coherent sentence for a few seconds. The Buckhead district alone has been booming with new development, and I've watched those deals go to other firms while we focused exclusively on residential properties. A whole untapped market has been sitting right under my nose.

When I can finally speak, I sputter, "How do I start, because we're obviously late and you know how I hate to be late."

Virgil smiles, sitting back. "I'll make a few phone calls. Set up a few meetings. We're on the verge of a whole new division of Donovan Luxury Real Estate."

* * *

"Commercial. Well that's new." Joseph muses out loud as he lounges at one end of the couch. His jacket is flung across the back of the couch and his shoes lay where he kicked them off when he came home. He's been working long hours since his promotion, so by the time he makes it home, he's beat. He hasn't even had the energy to change his clothes.

But when he asked me about my day, I couldn't wait to tell him about the conversation I'd had with Virgil earlier in the day. The excitement carried me through the afternoon and into the evening.

"Not new. But definitely about to boom and I want in." I give Imani a wide smile and tempt her with a spoonful of baby food—peas and carrots, which smells terrible, but she seems to love it. Her mouth opens and closes around the spoonful of greenish orange concoction, which goes down as fast as it goes in and her mouth opens again. Her tiny hands clap together in delight.

"I wish I could say I invented luxury home sales, but I didn't."

"Well, to be fair, who knew luxury residential existed before Donovan? How many firms out there were only selling to high end customers when you came along? Not many, right?"

I bob my head from side to side in slight agreement to Joseph's point. "I'm afraid I'll be caught with my pants down. I don't have enough agents as it is."

The last of the peas and carrots goes into Imani's mouth. I wipe her face, then her fingers and lift the tray from the high-chair and pick her up, carting her over to Joseph.

"Entertain your daughter while I check on dinner."

"Hi, sweet thing," he coos, his eyes lighting up when I set her on his lap. The exhaustion that lined his face moments ago melts away as he gazes at our daughter. "Come on over here and spit up on this expensive silk tie mommy bought me."

I round the corner into the kitchen, grabbing a couple of pot holders before pulling the oven door open, letting out steam and the rich aroma of melted cheese and spices.

"Might want to take that tie off. You know what we say... it'll happen—"

"Because we said it would happen. Already done."

Joseph appears in the doorway, sans tie, Imani happily

perched on his arm. His mahogany skin glows, his dark eyes wide and lively when they're on hers. He looks so handsome with a baby, I'd marry him all over again.

"I guess you haven't given any thought to our conversation."

My body goes rigid at the mention of the conversation I was hoping he'd forget about.

"You guess wrong. I did give it some thought. Plenty of thought." I busied myself with the enchiladas in the oven, then fluff the rice on the stove and give the black beans a stir. The wooden spoon scrapes against the pot with more force than necessary.

"Maxine, you were just talking about opening a new division at Donovan and hiring new agents. Doesn't sound like you're pulling back any time soon."

From the refrigerator, I pull out a bowl of salad I threw together the evening before and a few bottles of salad dressing. "No, it sure doesn't sound like that." My voice is tight, controlled.

With his free hand he cups my elbow and pulls so I have to turn around. His touch is gentle but insistent. "Are you trying to be funny, or are we having a conversation?"

"I'm trying to be funny. Because I don't want to have a conversation." I step around him, pulling plates and glasses from the cabinet. The clink of dishware punctuates the tension building between us. "Why don't you bathe her and put her to bed? By the time you're back down here, it'll be time to eat."

Joseph doesn't answer, nor does he move from his spot in the kitchen. I sense his eyes boring into my back as I pull out silverware and napkins and set two places at the island, where we take most of our meals. When we first moved into the new house, we ate in the formal dining room at the table that seats ten people. After a few weeks, it was ridiculous to sit in that huge room by ourselves, to listen to our voices bounce off the walls. One night, Joseph picked up his plate and mine and moved to the island. We've been eating there ever since.

Finally, he pushes out a long, loud sigh. "When I come back down here, I hope you'll have something more to say about this conversation than some flippant comments and cute stuff."

"I might. I might not." I turn, finally, and reach for Imani. "If you're not going to bathe her, I will. I have her on a schedule—"

"I've got her, Max," he snaps. "I'm going. I'm just saying..."

"I hear you, Joseph. Fine. We'll talk, but I don't think you you're going to like what you'll hear."

He glares at me for a beat, then turns and heads toward the stairs. I hear his footfalls turn into Imani's bedroom. In a few minutes I hear the water running for her bath.

My shoulders begin to drop, releasing the tension they're carrying. How can he think I would even consider giving up my business? For what? To sit at home and be Mrs. Joseph Glass? Join some clubs and volunteer full time?

Be the bitch at the PTA? *Tuh.*

I huff aloud, at no one, and head toward the wine fridge. I'm not producing milk anymore, so it's officially safe to drink. I pull a nice Pinot Gris from our stash and pop the cork.

I'm going to need some fortification.

I pour pale gold liquid into a glass because I can already predict the conversation that awaits me. The one where I'll have to choose between the life I've built and the life he seems to think I want.

four

* * *

AFTER DINNER, Malcolm snores in Daddy's lounger
while a basketball game plays on TV. I stand at the kitchen sink
washing our dishes. One of the perks of grilling is minimal
cleanup. Malcolm's empty bottles land in the recycling bin. I
wipe down the table and sweep the floor. I can't compete with
Debra's homemaking skills, but tonight my post-dinner
routine is unusually thorough.

I'm keeping busy to avoid thinking about her. What could
his ex-wife possibly want from Malcolm? He didn't seem
worried beyond the annoyance of hearing from her. I'm not
afraid of losing him to her; I hate that we have to deal with her
at all.

Unable to stand it anymore, I grab my phone from the
charger and open the group text that Maxine, Debra, and I
have maintained. It's barely functional—we haven't been in
the same room for months, relying on "say hi to whoever"
messages when we part.

Great minds think alike. Max and Debra had already been texting tonight.

Maxine: Joseph and I had a fight. I used to think fighting was so passionate. It's a drag when you're too tired for make-up sex.

Maxine: What are you two doing?

Debra: Last night, my daughter said the word FUPA and is worried about getting fat. Why can't we skip the teenage years?

Debra: And I was eavesdropping on Willard and heard something I probably shouldn't have.

Maxine: FUPA? What's that? And what did you hear? It's nothing bad is it?

Debra: Fat upper...

Debra: You know what? Google it. I'm not typing that in here.

Maxine: I don't think I want to know. But what did Willard say? And where the hell is Renee? What's she doing that's so important?

Debra: Malcolm. That's what she's doing. Hi Renee, whenever you see this waves

Debra: What did you and Joseph fight about?

Maxine: I'm too tired to type it. We need a brunch date!

Debra: I promised Willard we'd look at options for his office renovation. Yay, Lowe's.

Maxine: I was telling Renee this morning that maybe we need a change of venue. A different place, a different time.

Debra: You mean not having brunch at Ruby's anymore? I don't know if I want that.

Maxine: Ruby would hunt us down. But maybe drinks? I can swing by a place on my way home from work easier than I can be up and out of the house on a Saturday morning.

Debra: That's true. We could do a happy hour somewhere and be home at a reasonable hour.

Maxine: Or not, if I'm avoiding a conversation with my husband. Where is Renee! We need her to weigh in on this.

Now that I'm caught up, I join the conversation:

Renee: The TV is watching my man snore. I'm all for a happy hour. I need my girls like nobody's business.

Maxine: Then it's settled. I know just the place. I'll text you both the address. Can we meet up tomorrow? I'm desperate.

My shoulders sag with relief, so much that I feel embarrassed by my reaction. I'll table all my feelings, misgivings, and worries until tomorrow when I can see my girls. We'll figure this out. We always do.

five

DEBRA

"Have a seat, Mariah."

I gesture to the cushion at the other end of the small couch squeezed into the corner of my office. The couch is comfortable, chosen specifically for these moments. I find that people talk more easily in casual, relaxed settings rather than across a desk where I'd be looming over them.

Mariah practically collapses onto the couch, tucking one leg underneath her. She's thin, almost frail, with stringy hair. The shadows beneath her puffy eyes and her baggy clothes worry me. She looks like she hasn't been sleeping or eating properly.

"How's your dad doing?" I ask, reaching across the space between us to grasp her hand. Her cold fingers cling to mine as I watch her swallow hard, her throat bobbing with the effort.

"He had his first round of chemo last week. That's why I had to call in. He said he was fine, but then..." She shakes her head slowly, her gaze dropping to her lap. "Then he wasn't."

"Have the doctors given you any more news about his prognosis?"

Mariah shrugs, using the sleeve of her oversized hoodie to swipe at a tear crawling down her cheek. I reach for the box of Kleenex on the coffee table and place it between us. She pulls out a tissue, wipes away the tears that follow the first one, then dabs under her nose.

"We caught it early. Colon cancer is something lots of people overcome with treatment." She pauses, sniffling. Her eyes drift past me to fixate on the wall. "My dad seems hopeful. So I have to be hopeful too. I don't want to drag him down."

"No, of course not."

Conversations with Mariah have been difficult lately. It's been just her and her father for most of her life. He'd been feeling sick and run down for months. After constant pestering from Mariah, he finally made an appointment with his doctor. When the diagnosis came, it threw them both into a tailspin. Appointments, evaluations, surgery, then scheduling radiation and chemotherapy—all of it wreaked havoc on daily life in the Young household.

Marty would be devastated to learn that Mariah had been shirking her duties at ELCC to care for him. And Ms. Henry, who didn't know about Mariah's personal struggles, wouldn't tolerate an undependable employee for long. That's why I'd asked to meet with her today.

"I know I've been absent a lot," Mariah says, jumping ahead. "And I heard Ms. Henry was mad about last week. I went to her and apologized, but she didn't seem to accept my apology."

She averts her gaze to the floor, twisting her mouth to one side.

"You're dealing with so much right now," I say gently. "But these kids have lives that are unstable enough. This needs to be a place they can count on, which means I need staff I can count on. So I have to ask what we can do to make this better? I know you don't want to lose your job, and I don't want that either. But I also understand you want to be there for your dad. Do we need to change your schedule? Maybe you could go on the fill-in list, and we'd call you when we need someone—"

Her head snaps up, eyes wide with panic. "Oh no! I need more hours than that! I've been covering some bills so Dad can pay his hospital copays. I can't afford to make less."

"Okay, okay." I nod, understanding her predicament. "But I can't have you bailing on us at the last minute either. Ms. Henry told me you've used your last chance. Why haven't you told her what's going on? Or given me permission to share it with her?"

She sneers and rolls her eyes. "Every time I go in there to talk to her about something, she stares at me like I'm supposed to tell her why she should care about what I'm saying. She doesn't give a shit as long as I show up for work. She's not like you." Her voice softens. "I wish you had her job."

Mariah has no idea what a soothsayer she is. I've been thinking nonstop about stepping up to that plate for the exact reasons she just described. Eleanor Henry is an administrator, not a caregiver. There's a huge difference, and having come from an administrative background, I believe I could blend both roles successfully.

I make a mental note to speak with Eleanor this afternoon about being considered for the promotion.

Mariah slides across the couch and lays her head on my shoulder. Though she makes no sound, I feel her silent tears. Every few moments, she dabs at her nose with the tissue, her shoulders hitching slightly with each breath.

"I'm just so scared, Ms. Debra," she whispers. "I feel like maybe if I don't talk about it, it won't be real. Maybe talking about it makes it real. Maybe talking about how scared I am will make him get worse."

"That's human," I whisper, stroking her hair, still damp from her morning shower. "And completely normal. While I think Ms. Henry would still like to know what's going on with you, I won't tell her if you don't want me to. But anytime you need someone to talk to, you can come get me or call me. I'm always here for you. Okay?"

She sniffles, then sits up and moves back to her corner of the couch as if her crying spell never happened. It's remarkable how we don't allow ourselves a proper breakdown when we need one. I remember when I wouldn't let myself feel the pain of my crumbling marriage and lost job. It's a difficult habit to break.

"About my schedule," she says, composing herself. "Dad has chemo and radiation once a week, but on different days. The chemo days are rough right now, but his appointments are late afternoon. I love the after-school program, but I could try moving to mornings."

My eyebrows lift hopefully at this compromise. "You wouldn't have to completely switch to mornings. Just twice a week. Would that work?"

"I'll make it work," she says with determination. "I'm sorry again about the last-minute callouts. He's just... not used to it yet."

"I know, honey. Just give me a call when you know you can't make it, and I'll do my best to cover for you."

"But Ms. Henry said—"

"Let's make a deal," I say, extending my hand palm up. "You concern yourself with Martin Young. I'll concern myself with Ms. Henry. Deal?"

She smiles—probably for the first time all day and gives my hand a firm shake.

"Now get out of here. Your kids will be here any second."

After she slips out the door, I remain on the couch and allow myself a deep sigh. Both my parents are still living, but Maxine and I practically had to carry Renee through losing her mother. Her father's descent into Alzheimer's hasn't been easy either. I can't imagine facing what Mariah is dealing with. Especially if I were only twenty-three years old.

That afternoon, after all the after-school kids have arrived and checked into their activity rooms, the reading group has met to discuss their latest chapter, and I've finished my rounds, I tap on Ms. Henry's door. It's open, but only slightly— her version of an open-door policy.

"Debra," she says with an unusually warm greeting. She pulls her glasses from her nose and actually smiles. Knowing she's leaving ELCC must be lightening her mood; she's been almost pleasant lately. "Come in. Have a seat. How's everything?"

I step inside and close the door softly. "Just made the rounds. All's well." I take a seat and cross my legs, my Nine West flats dangling from my toes. I stifle a laugh, thinking how Maxine hates these shoes but they're comfortable and perfect for all the walking I do.

"I spoke with Mariah. I don't think we'll have any more issues with her calling out. She understands that if she can't be dependable, we can't keep her employed."

Eleanor seems pleased. She also doesn't seem remotely interested in why Mariah has been undependable. That's the key difference between us and how this office could operate differently with me in charge.

"And," I continue, "I wanted to revisit our conversation from last week. About your pending retirement."

She sits forward, resting her forearms on the desk and

clasping her fingers together. "Yes? You've given the idea some thought?"

"I have. And I'd like to throw my hat in the ring."

"You would?" she asks, which surprises me. She'd made it clear I didn't have much choice in the matter. My appearance in her office to formally accept being bullied into this process was supposed to be a mere formality.

"Do you honestly feel you're ready to assume a position like this again? In light of your... issues?"

I know she's being serious, but I find the question amusing. There are no handsome, hunky former football players on staff waiting to catch me in a vulnerable state and join me in breaking rules and risking our jobs. The closest we have is the head of janitorial services, and Jeffrey—a thirty-two-year-old with four young children—isn't exactly a temptation.

Besides, I'm in a completely different place than I was at Morningside. There's no pressure from a superintendent above me, no resentment from staff below me. I spend more time teaching than filling out forms, more time directing education than dictating goals for teachers and disciplining grown adults who don't meet them. And there's no competitive hostility with other school districts. ELCC works collaboratively with every city community center.

Willard and I are different too—in a much better place than before. With Willard so unhappy at Willoughby that he might quit, I want to be prepared to support our family the way he has all these years.

I hesitate, choosing diplomacy. "I'm nervous and you know why. It's a step into a role that feels designed with me in mind. I think I'd do well in this position, and if Dr. West will have me, I'll give it my best shot."

Her lips purse into thin slashes of garish red lipstick. She's quiet for so long that I worry she's changed her mind about recommending me. I prepare to backpedal, but she cuts me off.

"Very well," she says, picking up her glasses from their resting spot on her chest and sliding them back onto her nose. "I'll speak with Theodore this week and let you know the next steps. Thank you for coming in."

Eleanor returns to the document she's typing on her ultrathin laptop. The keys click softly for a few moments before her eyes dart back up to mine.

"Was there anything else, Debra? I have a grant application I'm trying to complete."

"Oh. No, I... that's it." Feeling dismissed, I rise from the chair and head toward the door.

"Debra."

I stop and turn. Without looking up from her screen or missing a keystroke, she says, "Come see me next Tuesday. I'll probably have some news for you then."

I leave her office and wait until I'm out of sight before leaning against the wall with a massive sigh. My heart hammers in my ears, and my hands are trembling. Am I really doing this?

I take a deep breath to steady myself, willing my heartbeat to slow and shaking out my hands until they stop quivering.

Yes. You're doing this, Debra. It's about time you took a step forward.

* * *

"Don't we have a rule about letting Maxine choose places?"

"If we don't, we need to institute one," grumbles Renee, her eyes scanning the swanky, leather-bound, crystal-laden establishment where we'd agreed to meet. "A drink is about all I can afford in this place."

We wander through the waiting area of Minks, a steak-house and rooftop cigar bar in the heart of Buckhead, Atlanta's business and financial district. The name sounds familiar, but I've never been inside. As usual, I'd only set foot in a place like this if Maxine was paying.

Through the front windows, I spot the Maserati—stark white and unmistakable—pull up to the valet stand. Maxine emerges from the car, stylish as ever in white palazzo trousers, heels, and a blue-and-white blouse. She hands her keys to the valet and strides inside to join us.

Renee and I parked in a lot down the street and walked half a block to the restaurant in our jeans and casual tops.

"Girls!" Max gushes, arms spread wide.

Renee and I both fall into her embrace for what might be the loudest, most dramatic group hug we've ever shared. I feel the need for this night in my shoulders and chest. I see it on Renee's face and hear it in her voice.

When we separate, I struggle not to get emotional. Menopause is turning my body into a rollercoaster. I suppress my tears by giving Maxine a not-so-gentle tap on the arm.

"Why do you always do this, woman?"

"Do what?" Max asks innocently, already pulling a Kleenex from her purse for Renee, who is predictably sniffling.

"Look at this place! Renee and I can barely afford to walk in here, let alone drink."

"Oh, hush, Debra. It's happy hour. Second, we're going up to the roof to use the Kincaid discount." Maxine rolls her eyes and pulls open the door leading to the restaurant and the elevator to the rooftop.

We step inside, and Max presses the "R" button. The glass cube begins its smooth ascent.

Over her shoulder, she mumbles, "I just knew you would have something to say. You two are so predictable and basic."

"Basic? Excuse me, Miss Head-to-Toe Prada."

"Gucci, thank you."

I nudge Renee, standing directly behind Maxine. "If I knock her out, you'll take care of Imani, right?"

Renee's face lights up with mischief. "As her favorite auntie, I could not possibly deny my lil' doo wop chocolate drop."

"Favorite? Imani loves her Auntie Debra. Look, don't you start. You can get it too. You know my hormones are raging."

"Are you getting any benefit out of that?" Renee asks with a sly grin. "Or should I ask if Willard is getting any benefit?"

"Don't sound like it," chirps Maxine. "Somebody needs her knees pinned to her ears. Not that Willard the Prude knows anything about that—"

I gasped. "Maxine Elise! I told you that in confidence."

"Debra, please. You can look at Willard and know he specializes in missionary."

"Why don't y'all ever talk about sex with me?" Renee asks.

Maxine turns to glare at Renee over her shoulder, then turns back to watch the numbers above the elevator slowly change. "Because you don't offer up any info. And any time we even hint at Malcolm's bedroom prowess, you get so embarrassed, you slide off the chair to the floor."

The elevator doors slide open to reveal a beautiful space filled with white-clothed tables—some in the open air, others under glass enclosures. Overhead, R&B music thrums from speakers at the perfect volume. In seconds, I can tell Minks is where Atlanta's young, Black, and upwardly mobile come to see and be seen.

A hand shoots into the air, and a deep voice calls out, "Debra! Renee!"

My attention is drawn to a group of men at a corner table,

puffing cigars in the open-air section. Their jackets are off, sleeves rolled up, ties probably stuffed into pockets.

"Gibson!" I smile at the familiar handsome face and hurry over. He stands, pushing back his chair to receive the enthusiastic hug he can't escape. When I release him, he nods to Renee and Maxine, who don't assault him the way I did.

"It's ridiculous how long it's been. How are you? And Vanessa and the girls?"

"Well, since Diya's legal issues were resolved, I haven't had reason to visit the center. But we're doing great—everyone's great." He beams with the unmistakable pride of a man in love with his new family. A year ago, he won a highly contested divorce for one of Maxine's agents, Vanessa. He won her heart in the process, and her daughters adore him too.

"Vanessa is selling houses like crazy, and the girls are growing like weeds. I swear we're shopping every few months."

"Marilyn usually brings the girls to the bookstore when they visit their uncle at Sam's," Renee says. "They really are tall —carbon copies of Vanessa."

"Yeah, they love Gladwell's."

"We're starting a book club for kids. I know they'll want to join."

"They sure will. I'll let them know."

"Vanessa and Gib just closed on their new house in the city," Maxine adds with barely concealed pride.

"With help from you, no doubt?" I tease.

"No doubt," she shoots back. "When a Kincaid calls, Donovan answers."

She pauses to pull a stack of business cards from her shoulder bag, handing one to each man at the table. "Donovan Luxury Realty. When you're ready to upgrade, give us a call. Ask Sylvia about me. Then tell her to call me; that mansion she and Judge Kincaid are living in is too big, and they both know it."

The table groans in unison. Gibson laughs. "We've been trying to get Mother and Judge to downsize for years. Maybe you can chat with her—you know, high-powered business-woman to high-powered businesswoman."

"Don't flirt with me, Gibson. I'm married, and you're nearly down the aisle yourself."

He laughs again, crossing his arms over his broad chest. "Just a few months away, in fact."

"Well!" I sigh, clasping my hands together while my eyes involuntarily drift to the bar's alcohol selection. I quickly avert my gaze—I'm not truly tempted, but still. "We have drinks and girl time waiting. We'll let you gentlemen return to your cigars."

With quick hugs and promises to catch up soon, we make our way to a shaded table at the roof's edge with a stunning sunset view of Atlanta's skyline.

Maxine, who had stopped at the bar, is the last to sit down. "First round is on me, ladies," she announces. "Debra, I got you a zero-proof red."

"Thank you," I say, grateful that she remembered I've been alcohol-free since my accident. My car was totaled, and I nearly lost my job, but if there's a silver lining, it's that the inci-dent brought me back into my home and convinced Willard that our marriage deserved another chance.

"Who wants to start?"

"You go first," Renee says. "Then I'll know whether my issues are ridiculous or not."

"Why would—" Maxine huffs. "No, you go first, Renee. Malcolm isn't fucking up, is he?"

"No, not at all. He's perfectly happy with how things are."

"So what's the problem?"

"She doesn't want him to be perfectly happy, obviously," I observe.

"I just..." Renee pauses as glasses arrive at the table. When the waitress leaves, she continues. "I've been thinking a lot about what comes next for us. The forever part. Are we going to live in my parents' house, plant a garden, and grill out every weekend, just the two of us, forever? Because that's cool and all, but—"

"You're looking for something more permanent," Maxine finishes, lifting her glass and taking a sip, rolling her eyes as she swallows. "Well, from the trenches of the newly married, it's not all sunshine and roses."

My heart sinks at the first hint of trouble in Maxine's marriage. Joseph was exactly what she needed when he appeared in her life. She fought him every step of the way, but when she finally gave in, it was beautiful to witness. Joseph brings out the Maxine that Renee and I have known since childhood—the side she rarely shows anyone else.

"The honeymoon isn't over already, is it, Max?"

"Only one of us can fall apart at a time," she mutters, taking another sip. She seems genuinely troubled, making me anxious to hear the full story. "And it's Renee's turn. But to answer your question, no. It's still blissful as fuck in the Glass household. We're just having a communication issue. Anyway..."

Her gaze shifts back to Renee. "Have you and Malcolm ever discussed the future? Have you defined what happens next?"

Renee lifts one shoulder and twists her lips to the side. "Not in so many words. He acts like he plans on us being together long-term. I mean, he moved in with me and Daddy. Helped me get Daddy into Golden Rays. Helped me paint, redecorate, he's obsessive about the yard work. He talks about expanding the bookstore..."

She exhales a frustrated breath as her shoulders slump. "All I can think about is wearing a white dress, getting a big-ass rock, and changing my name. I see Imani and I want fat babies with his eyes and my dimples. Am I terrible? Should I not complain about this?"

I laugh along with Maxine—not at Renee, but in sympathy with her plight.

"Honey, no. It seems like he's in it for the long haul. I understand not wanting to waste time but remember Malcolm's big on action and small on words."

"Sure is," Maxine mutters under her breath. Her eyes widen when she realizes we heard her. "I'm just saying."

"You wouldn't have heard those words anyway, Maxine." I turn back to Renee. "I think you need to talk to him. Closed mouths don't get fed."

"That was the plan last night. I made dinner, got him pie from Ruby's, all but fixed the man a martini. But then he came home grumpy over a phone call from his ex-wife."

"Shit Renee! You should have opened with that!" Maxine leans forward, wine glass aloft. "The hell did she want?"

"She left a message asking him to call. But they never talk. Ever. So her calling means something. He wants to find out what's happening in up there before he calls back because he hates walking into traps. But here's the thing—last night, he said he dodged a bullet—" Renee used air quotes around the term—"when he divorced her. In his words, 'the whole marriage thing—I'm not going down that road again.'"

"Oh." I sit back, trying to mask my disappointment. "What did he mean by that?"

"If I have to hunt down Malcolm Brooks and beat some sense into him, I will," Maxine declares. "Because I know he remembers me telling him not to hurt you."

"He's not—"

"And what does his marriage to that raggedy woman have to do with you?" I ask, feeling my temper rise. "Every relationship is different, especially when you learn your lessons and do better."

"Y'all stop." Renee raises both hands, palms out. Maxine and I immediately shut our mouths. "I appreciate the posse, but he's not hurting me. He has no idea I'm ready for more. And I'm thinking now isn't the time to bring it up. He's genuinely upset about hearing from her, and I don't want his feelings about her to taint our conversation—especially when I need to admit I can't stop thinking about getting pregnant and having a little Brooks baby."

"You should just get pregnant," Maxine suggests before draining her glass.

I glare at her.

"What? It solves so many problems. Then he has to think about marriage and family."

"Is that how you trapped Joseph? You got pregnant?"

Maxine purses her lips and glares back at me. "I did not trap Joseph, thank you very much. He is supremely happy being married to me and fathering our daughter."

"Anyway, before you two start snipping at each other..." Renee leans forward with a thoughtful expression. "Things with Malcolm are fine. Great, even. I keep telling myself this. We have no issues between us. Even our disagreements end well. Maybe it's too early to worry about it. I feel like... I need a sign."

She glances pointedly at Maxine. "And I don't need that sign to be a plus on a pregnancy test."

"I don't want you copying me anyway. Do your own thing."

"Do you think this has anything to do with Bernard's decline?" I ask gently. "Maybe losing the last of your immediate family has you searching for something to hold onto?"

Renee contemplates this for several long seconds. Then, softly, she admits, "Maybe. You know, even if I had a baby tomorrow, Daddy would never know his grandch—"

She bursts into tears before finishing the sentence.

Maxine and I leap from our seats and assume our usual formation—arms tight around her until she calms down.

Maxine tucks napkins into her hands, making her laugh through tears when she reminds her to dab, dab, dab.

Renee takes a deep breath and dries her eyes.

"Have you considered therapy?" I ask.

She pauses, looking at me warily. "You think I'm crazy? That I've got real problems?"

"No, I think you need to talk to someone. Get everything out in the open. Especially so you don't expect Malcolm to fill the void Bernard can't."

"She has a point, Renee," Maxine says. "Therapy isn't just for crazy people. You need a head doctor like you need a pussy doctor."

"Maxine," I scold, trying not to laugh.

"Point out the lie!"

"It's not a lie. You just don't have to be so—"

"Do you have one? A therapist?" Renee asks Maxine.

Maxine's mouth drops open. "Well... not... no. But I'm just saying. Debra still sees a therapist. Right, Deb?"

"We're talking about you, Maxine."

"Technically, we're talking about Renee. But I'll tell you what—Renee and I might go halfsies on a therapist because..." She sighs deeply and shakes her head. "This man the Lord gave me..."

"Alright, lady," I say, folding my arms and leaning onto the table. "Out with it. You sound stressed. Spill."

Maxine shakes her head slowly. "Stressed is not even the word."

six

MAXINE

Not for nothing, but I was hoping Debra and Renee would unload first, so I could get out all of my barbs and well-meaning advice and they'd be too tired to lecture me about what I need to do with Joseph. How I should think about how strong my drive is and maybe a man could feel intimidated by who I am as a person.

And they would be right... to an extent.

It takes a lot to be me. I like being me, but not even me is me. Debra and Renee know that, which is the only reason I still have friends. The facade I put on every day is my armor, built to face the male-dominated career I've chosen. I've loved kicking the door in. But maybe my marriage isn't the place to be strong, to kick in doors.

"What do you mean, stressed isn't the word? What's going on with you and Joseph? Is it serious?" Debra leans in, concern etched across her face.

"Sort of?" I motion for more wine for Renee and me. Debra

asks for sparkling water with lemon. That's such a Debra thing to ask for.

I continue once the waitress steps away, the city lights beginning to twinkle in the darkening sky behind us. "You know, when Joseph and I met, he had some work to do—"

"He was nowhere near the Maxine Standard," Debra interjects, dry as desert sand.

"Correct." I point a finger at her. "To be fair, he knew when he started dating me that I was used to a certain kind of man. I'm happy to report that Joseph Xavier Glass has put in work. He's making moves and serious money. He's really happy, and things can only get better from here."

I pause to exhale, the weight of what I'm about to say sitting heavy on my chest.

"Aw shit," says Debra, already sensing what's coming.

"Aw, shit?" asks Renee, glancing between us.

"In Max's world, this means her beau or love interest starts to get jealous and tries to compete with her or tame her. And it doesn't end well."

"That's an understatement," I add, agreeing. "I am the same person I was when I met him, but now we're on even footing. With bonuses and profit sharing, he's even a little bit ahead."

I feel my lip curl involuntarily. "And now he thinks he's hot shit, head of the household that he runs things, and—"

"Nobody runs Maxine," we chant in unison.

I laugh aloud, the tension in my shoulders loosening slightly. "I must have said that a time or two."

"Or a thousand," Debra mutters.

"He's got this idea... rather, a senior partner at the investment firm has been putting these ideas in his head that he should have a devoted, prim little wife standing dutifully behind her husband. I can have a cute little job or whatever, but I should really be focused on my family and our home. Maybe wear some pearls and volunteer at charities and whatever—"

"So, Charlotte Rogers, then?" Debra says, referencing an old nemesis.

"You know that is exactly who I thought of when he floated that idea to me. I told him how I felt about all of that. He said that was silly and it wouldn't be like that."

Renee laughs, her eyes brightening for the first time since we sat down. "You can't be tied down like that. You have never had a *little* job. Imagine you mopping floors with a smile—"

"I mean, you just said the word pussy all out in the open. That's not a prim and proper banker's wife at all," Debra adds.

"Exactly my point, Debra."

"Does Prada make maid outfits?" Debra asks, smirking. "Maybe you should get one. Put all your jewelry on—"

"Add some Chris Lous, and that'll get me laid, but it won't prove my point. Renee is right, though. I don't have anything against women who want to stay home with their babies and cater to their men. If I was the kind of woman who could be happy doing that, I'd sell my interests in Donovan in a hot second and join the life."

I shrug a shoulder. "But I'm not. I was hoping he'd catch the hint, but he's pushing it so hard that I've been avoiding talking to him. And last night, things came to a head."

"Hold up. Refills coming." Renee tips her head toward the approaching waitress.

I wait until she places our drinks, then order an appetizer. I sense a few more rounds approaching and need to soak up some alcohol before going home.

"So last night?" Debra prods, leaning forward, her refreshed drink halfway to her mouth.

"Well, let me back up. Yesterday, Virgil and I had a really

exciting conversation about a possible new division at Donovan—high end commercial real estate. Not plain brown buildings, but classy joints for the people who live at the top. We both think it's a great idea, something I want to jump into with both feet, but my agents are already tapped. I would need to hire and train new agents to work this new line. I came home very excited, chatting away, and my husband..."

I sigh with a roll of my eyes.

"Popped your balloon," Debra finishes. "While you're out here threatening to knock some sense into Malcolm, you might start with your husband."

"That's why I said it's not all sunshine and roses over here. In his mind, we've had this conversation about me pulling back from the business a few times, and he considers it a done deal."

"He can't *honestly* mean for you to quit your job and stay at home." Renee's eyes widen with disbelief.

"I don't know what he means, but he's sounding real Neanderthal right now, and the more we talk about it, the less I want to talk about it. I'll tell you something," I say, the nail of one finger tapping against the table. "I love that man with everything in me. I love our child. But I'm not shrinking so he can impress those white men. I worked too hard to get where I am to set it aside for a male ego."

Debra sighs, swirling her wine. Though it is zero proof, I can't tell. She seems a little looser and lighter. "Willard is getting some of the same. People above him telling him how much time to spend in the office, the right things to say and do to become partner. It's been years of them dragging him around on a leash."

"I'm sure changing his office hours and moving most of his work home didn't go over well with the higher-ups," said Renee.

"At first it did. They claim to be all about work-life balance and family first. But after a year, they started nagging him about face time and taking on more work, even though he's billing more than everyone else. The other night, I overheard him on the phone. They're basically saying he's not eligible for partner if he doesn't increase his time in the office."

"How do you feel about that, Debra?" asks Renee.

"I love having Willard at home. He's still working six days a week. What will being in the office do but give them one more face to look at? I mean... if he gets to be partner, fine. He'll go back to the office. But he's talking about leaving the firm."

"What?" I screech, popcorn shrimp suspended between my fingers and mouth. "Willard has been at that firm forever."

Debra shakes her head, giving Renee and me a sad smile. "He said it out loud, on the phone with...whoever he was talking to. And frankly, if that's what he wants, I'm behind him. But it means I need to make some moves of my own."

"Meaning? You're not leaving ELCC, are you?"

"Not at all. In fact, Ms. Henry called me into her office the other day to tell me she's retiring. And she wants me to apply for her job."

"Wooooowwww," Renee and I both say, then glance at each other and laugh.

"Yep," says Debra, laughing too. "That is exactly what I said. Wow, do I want to get back into administration? Wow, do I trust myself in that situation again? Wow, what is Willard going to think?"

"Do you think you have a chance at getting it? Do you have to apply, or... what happens?"

"Oh, I'm sure I'll apply and interview. The decision is up to Dr. West; he's our liaison with the city and works with the Advisory Board. It'll be up to him to convince them that I'm a good fit. I'm pretty nervous about that..."

"Because... maybe there hasn't been enough time since..."

"Yeah," Debra says, then presses her lips together. She hasn't quite made it over the hump of losing her job, nearly losing her marriage and sullying her reputation. "I don't want them to feel like I'm coming straight out of prison, asking for a high-ranking job. I did my time, I re-entered society—"

"If you don't stop talking like you just got off an eighteen month bid over there." I roll my eyes at her, which hasn't had an effect on her since we were teenagers, but I do it anyway out of habit. "But you're right; you got a new job, and you've been kicking ass at it. I'm going to start making a list of people who need a talking-to. My husband is at the top of it."

"Oh, I'm so sorry, Maxine! We didn't finish talking about Joseph—"

"Don't worry about it," I say, waving off her concern. "Mr. Glass will be alright. If he wants to stay married, he will wake up. Sylvia Kincaid made sure we have an ironclad prenup. He's not getting shit in the divorce."

Somebody always starts it. The giggles. It's usually Renee, and then Debra, and then I'm laughing because they're laughing. By the time we settle down, I'm not feeling as tense and rage filled as I did when I sat down. I know, in my heart, that this is exactly what I needed.

"So you're going for the promotion, right? Does Willard know?"

"I talked with Eleanor today and told her I'm interested. I'll talk to Willard over the weekend. This could mean a serious flip for our family, one where I'm the breadwinner who carries the insurance and the 401(k), and Willard buys the groceries and pays the paperboy."

"Well, make sure he does the dishes in his lil' maid outfit with all his bling on."

"I don't know about all that..." Renee cringes. "He doesn't have hips for those little dresses."

"You're right," Debra and I agree simultaneously.

"He wouldn't do that anyway," adds Debra with a chuckle. "Although...I recently got him to have sex with the lights on."

"How risqué. Is therapy still going okay?" I ask her. "Do you think Willard will be worried about you basically returning to administration?"

"Still going. It's working so far," she finishes with a tight smile.

Renee and I pause, exchanging glances.

"Debra..."

"What? Nothing! I promise. Scout's honor." She puts two peace signs in the air. "I'm just starting to wonder when we graduate from therapy."

"Oh. That's a good question. When do you stop going?"

Debra shrugs a shoulder. "I guess when we both feel like we don't need it anymore. And I don't think we're there yet." She lifts her glass and takes a full-mouth gulp of wine like it actually has alcohol in it.

My watch vibrates with a notification. I roll my wrist to check my text messages.

> JXG: Any idea of your ETA?

> JXG: Not rushing you at all. Bath and bedtime are coming up. Wait or go for it?

"Go," orders Renee. She nudges my shoulder with her fingertips. "It's Joseph, right? Imani is screaming her head off and he needs reinforcements?"

"No, she's fine. But it's about to be bath time, and she loves baths, and I haven't seen her all day..." I pause, looking at my very best friends in the world. "Will you guys really let me run off to be with my baby?"

"And that man that you created her with..." adds Debra, laughing.

"Get out of here, Maxine." Renee pulls my bag from its post on the back of my chair and slides it onto my shoulder as I stand. I reach into the bag to pull out my wallet and hand a card to Renee.

"Put everything on this. I'll get it from you tomorrow."

"Ooh, platinum AmEx. I'll bring you some coffee in the morning, your treat. Malcolm will be in the yard, and you know how that kicks up my allergies."

"I'm so jealous that you two live around the corner from each other again," Debra says, pouting.

"Sounds like you need to convince Willard that Decatur is greater and come on down!" I laugh, then push my chair in. "It was great to see you girls. Let's set up a brunch soon. I don't want Ruby hunting me down."

"It's a plan. Now go, that baby is waiting."

I haven't flown out of a place so fast since the night my water broke and Joseph panicked, dragging me through Chops Steakhouse, not realizing it could still be hours before Imani would arrive.

In minutes, I reach the valet stand and shove my ticket at the attendant. While he runs to retrieve my car, I text Joseph.

> MaxGlass: Go slow. I'm on my way.

> JXG: Slowing our roll

I chuckle at his attempt at humor. At least he wasn't snapping at me. He'd never really been the kind to drag out a fight. Moreover, he simply expected his wishes to be followed and was surprised when they weren't. Must be one of those first-born characteristics.

As an only child, I'd never had to consider anyone's word or opinion but Inell's, and even she wasn't one to lay down the law. I had entirely too much free rein, entirely too early. I'm still learning, years into this serious, committed, lifelong relationship thing, that my opinion isn't the only one that matters. Unfortunately, Joseph is learning this too.

The Maserati rolls to a stop in front of me, and I'm poised to hop in, cash tip ready.

"Sweet ride, Miss," the valet gushes. "Really smooth on pavement, and she takes corners like a dream. You ever take her out on the open road? You know, give her some—"

I shove a few dollars into his shirt pocket and hop into the car. I don't have time for some random to drool over the car. My baby is getting older by the second, and I need to witness every single moment.

* * *

"Did you notice how she knew which bath toy was the yellow one, the red one, the green one?"

Joseph practically glows as he moves around our bathroom, picking up Imani's discarded clothing. She's in her crib across the hall, out like a light for the moment. A hot bath, a cute onesie, her favorite blankie, and Daddy's soothing voice reading her a bedtime story work like an elixir. Lately, she's been grumpy because she's teething, but he can always get her down for the night.

"I noticed that," I comment, leaning against the doorjamb, watching him move about the room. "She's so smart. Inell has all kinds of smart kid toys over there."

"That's why we need to already be thinking about where to

send her for preschool. I don't want her coddled by teachers who'll just let her sit and watch YouTube Kids all day. We can hire a teenager to watch her for that."

"Mmmhmm," I hum. Joseph gets into these rants about the level of life he wants our daughter to live, as if I would have it any other way. "She's already on the list for Carlisle Montessori. I met with the headmaster when I was still pregnant. I got him a great deal on the house he bought. He owes me."

"But maybe Carlisle isn't the best. We should look around."

I scoff as if I wouldn't know the best schools and have connections to all of them. Carlisle topped my list before Imani was a twinkle in my eye. Language immersion, a high concentration on the arts, state-of-the-art facilities and classroom tools, a wide and varied mix of students and faculty that were elite educators, not harried, newly graduated teachers so new to the district that the ink had barely dried on their teaching licenses.

Not that I begrudge Debra or her colleagues but watching her go through her ordeal with the school district, the teacher she had an affair with, and that shrew on the PTA who tried to get her fired taught me some things about public education. I have no intention of throwing my baby to those wolves.

"Trust me, Joseph. They make the list of the best in the country every year."

I push off of the doorjamb and move into the bedroom. I hadn't changed out of my clothes when I got home, just kicked off my shoes and headed to the bathroom. I start undressing now, pulling at my blouse and loose, flowy pants, tossing them into a canvas drawstring bag. My closet is dry-cleaning only for the most part. Joseph likes his shirts, jackets, and slacks starched and pressed, so he has his own bag.

"I'm just saying," he continues, "it's never too early to plan for her future." He dumps Imani's outfit and used towels into a separate bag. Everything that wasn't dry-cleaned went to the laundry service, where it was washed, dried, folded, and delivered without me having to lift a finger. I haven't done laundry in the traditional sense in many years. Joseph rolled his eyes at my lifestyle when we met, but now he's so used to it, he falls right into step.

"And I'm saying that I hear you and I agree and we already have a leg up. She's nine months old, and she's already pre-enrolled in a premier private academy. Her college fund has been set up since she was an embryo. Handmade baby food, all-natural vegan products from diapers to stuff for her hair, Baby Mozart, all the infant learning tools. Stop lecturing me like I'm slacking."

Joseph pauses and pushes out a shallow breath. "I wasn't lecturing, Maxine. More talking out loud. Keeping the thought top of mind. Not for you. For me." He crosses the room, coming up behind me and sliding large, warm hands around my waist.

I resist the urge to cringe and twist away from him. I love his touch, but my face is still as full as when I was full term. I have baby weight that hasn't budged; my size six dresses are just languishing in my closet. He doesn't seem to notice, though, as his hands continue their journey, one going north toward my breasts, the other south, past the band of my sensible cotton panties. His lips dust my neck and shoulders; I shiver as goosebumps spread across my skin like wildfire.

He knows good and well what my hot spots are and he's hitting them, one at a time and then all at once.

"How are the girls?"

"They're alright," I tell him, my voice suddenly husky. "It was nice to see them. It's been a while."

"Mmhmm," he hums, the vibration sending another shockwave through me. He steps in closer so he's pressed against me, and I feel him swell. "Glad you got a chance to spend time with them. Sorry to rip you away, but I knew you wouldn't want to miss her tonight."

I turn around, forcing him to stop groping my body, stretching my arms until they rest on his shoulders. "You're right," I tell him, plopping a kiss on his lips. "I wouldn't have. And they understood. Even pushed me out of the restaurant so I could be here."

He chuckles. His taut belly bounces against my soft one. I vow again, like I do every Monday morning, to get back on my self-care regimen. Exercise. Healthy eating. Sleep.

Whatever, my brain argues. *Oreos taste amazing at 3 AM when you're up with the baby.*

"About last night..." he starts. His eyes narrow, and a wrinkle forms in the skin of his forehead.

"Let's leave last night where it is, hmm?"

"I don't want to leave things between us hanging in the air."

"Nothing's hanging, Joseph. Let's just give it a break. You didn't put our daughter to bed and get me all fired up to restart the fight we had last night, did you?"

His brows slowly rise and the wrinkle melts away. "All fired up, are you?"

"You know it doesn't take much. Can we just enjoy each other for a little bit? We can fight tomorrow."

seven

RENEE

The bedroom is still dark when I feel Malcolm slip out of bed. I lay still, eyes closed, listening to the familiar sounds of his morning routine—the soft padding of his feet across the carpet, the gentle click of the bathroom door, the rush of water as he showers.

I've barely slept. My mind was too busy replaying our conversation from the night before. When I arrived home after a Gladwell staff meeting, Malcolm was sitting in the kitchen, his laptop open on the table, a deep frown etched on his face.

"Hey," I said, hanging my keys on my designated hook and dropping my purse on the table. "Is everything okay?"

He looked up, his eyes clouded. "Charlene called again," he said without preamble. "I picked up before I realized who it was."

My stomach clenched at the mention of her name. I grabbed a chair, pulled it out and sat in it. "And? What does she want?"

"The business is being acquired by one of the biggest Security firms on the East Coast. They've been expanding, buying up smaller operations to bring under their umbrella. Anyway, they've been digging into the paperwork and it looks like she didn't properly dissolve my minority stake when she took over. I still own five percent on paper."

"How is that possible?" I asked. "I thought you gave up your stake in the business."

"I did. There was so much chaos when I left—my mother dying, her affair, signing the house over to her, me just wanting to get the hell out of DC. I never followed up on the paperwork. I signed some things, but she was supposed to file them. Apparently she never did."

"And now?"

Malcolm sighs, rubbing his temples. "The lawyers from the acquiring firm need me to sign off on the deal since I'm still legally part owner. If I don't, the deal falls apart and she's threatening to sue me for damages."

I bristle at the thought of Charlene inserting herself back into our lives. Over money.

He looks at me, his expression pained. "I'm sorry, Renee. I never meant for my past to crop up again like this."

"So she can send the papers here, you sign them and send them back."

"The deal closes Monday and she's worried I'll hold them and ask for more money."

This bitch. I saw why Malcolm couldn't wait to get away from her and didn't want to be in a room with her again.

"Does that face mean you're trying to figure out when you can go up there?"

"Yeah. I was looking at flights to go up, take care of business and come back." He tapped the space bar on his laptop. The screen lit up, illuminating the Delta Airlines page. "I can go up Friday morning. Take the first flight out, handle the meeting and paperwork. Maybe drop in on my dad and my sister. Be back Friday evening. Saturday morning at the latest."

Now, as morning light begins to poke through the blinds, I hear Malcolm moving around the bedroom. I roll over, no longer able to pretend to be asleep.

He pauses while buttoning a crisp white dress shirt and looks over his shoulder. "Hey. I thought I was being quiet. I didn't mean to wake you up."

"You didn't." I yawn, pushing myself up against the head-board, drawing the sheet with me and fluffing the pillows behind me. "Years of having to listen for my dad stumbling around looking for the bathroom means I sleep light. What time is your flight tomorrow?"

"Six thirty." He sits on the edge of the bed, reaching for his watch on the nightstand. "If all goes well, I can be at my sister's for lunch with my dad, on the way back home by six. I'll be a little late for dinner."

"I can drive you to the airport."

"No need to get you up that early. I've already booked a car service." He leans over, kisses my forehead. "You okay? You were tossing and turning all night."

I shrug. "A lot on my mind these days."

"Hmmm. Anything you can talk about?"

"Just...life." I shrug. "The bookstore. Daddy and his care." I pause, rolling my eyes up to his. "You going to DC to breathe the same air as your ex-wife."

Malcolm's eyes catch mine and hold them. "You know there's nothing to worry about with Charlene, right?"

"Logically, yes. I know." But the truth is, I don't. Not completely.

This woman shared his life, his bed, his name. She also betrayed him in the worst possible way, but that didn't mean the connection between them was entirely severed. The most toxic relationships can be the most addictive and the hardest to fully escape.

"It's strictly business," he continues. "I'm going up there to sign papers, see my dad and come home to the love of my life."

"Tell me anything," I say...but I'm smiling. I go so soft for this big burly man being sweet to me.

He studies me for a moment longer, then checks his watch again. "I do have to get going. Since I'm out on Friday, I have work to get out of the way. And Brent has a staff meeting at eight."

"Go. I love you. I'll see you tonight."

He kisses me again, this time on the lips, then grabs his jacket from the closet and heads for the door. I wait until I hear the garage door open and close, then the sound of the Denali engine fading as he drives away.

Only then do I allow myself to fall back against the pillows, my mind racing with thoughts I don't want to entertain.

Do I trust Malcolm? With my life.

Do I trust Charlene? Not even a little.

After a while, I throw off the covers and pad to the bath-room, turning the shower as hot as I can stand it. I step under the scalding spray in my shower bonnet and try to let the water sear away my doubts and insecurities.

It's that she's his ex-wife.

Ex. Wife. She got to wear the ring and have the ceremony and sign the papers and stand next to Malcolm and pledge her love to him.

I tilt my head back, letting the water course over my face, my eyes squeezed shut against the sting. I can't let her get to me. Not now, not after all this time. Malcolm and I have built a life together, a partnership based on love, trust, and mutual respect. She gave up her claim to him long ago.

I'm the happiest I've ever been and all I want is everything she threw away.

* * *

"We could expand the Young Adult section by several feet," Lexie suggests, gesturing to the far wall of the bookstore. "Move these shelves forward, create a cozy nook in the back with beanbags and a little table. The teens would love it."

I force myself to concentrate on Lexie's enthusiasm despite the anxiety gnawing at my stomach. "That could work. But we'd need to make sure it doesn't cut into the walkway too much."

"People should still be able to get through." Lexie tilts her head, studying me. "You okay, Renee? You seem...I don't know. Something."

"I'm okay. Just tired. Didn't sleep well."

"I thought those days were over when you moved your dad out."

"Like I told Malcolm this morning, it's muscle memory, I guess."

"Muscle memory... and worrying about him seeing his ex-wife."

I wave a hand dismissively. "Have you talked to any of the kids about book club yet? Do we have interest?"

Her face lights up. "Oh, God, yes. I've got six kids tentatively on board. And honestly, I think once we start, more will join. I was thinking they could meet right after school on Tuesdays or Wednesdays? Betty offered to provide snacks."

"She isn't providing them for free," I mutter. Betty has super hero hearing and would have an attitude if she knew we were talking about her. "Make sure you give her a budget— don't let her decide how much to charge us. And poll the kids to get any dietary restrictions. I can't be held responsible if someone eats gluten and they have an allergy."

"For sure. Also, we have a ton of local authors. We could reach out to some, maybe pick one of their books once a quarter, do some Q&As. Ooh! I bet the kids would love a book signing just for their age group."

Lexie's enthusiasm is so contagious, she really lifts my spirits. "Let's start with the club itself, see how it goes, then we can expand. But I love that idea. My mom used to have authors in here often. It's about time we got back to that."

"Great!" She glances at her watch. "Speaking of signings, UPS should be here soon with those books from Amistad. I need to make space in the storage room. They said they were sending a bunch."

"Thanks, Lexie."

As she walks away, I pull out my phone to check the time. I have a standing appointment to visit Daddy at Golden Rays and I don't like to be late. It's critical that I get time in before he begins to sundown.

Usually I look forward to these visits, despite how difficult they can be. Today, I'm grateful for the distraction.

Grabbing my purse from my office, I check out with Lexie and head out to my car. The drive is a familiar one now, though it never gets easier. Every visit is a reminder of how much has changed.

Golden Rays Assisted Living Facility is a sprawling complex with beautifully maintained grounds, gardens and walking paths for the residents who are able to enjoy them. The memory care unit, where Daddy lives, is in a separate wing with a secure entrance and twenty-four-hour care from aides like Jessie.

I sign in at the front desk, greet the receptionist and make my way down the familiar corridor to Daddy's room. The walls are lined with artwork created by the residents—colorful abstracts, simple landscapes, collages made in art therapy sessions.

"Well look who it is! Hey, Renee!"

Jessi's face breaks into a broad smile as she rushes down the hall toward me. She adjusts the golden rod sweatshirt with the Golden Rays logo over the left breast before enveloping me in a hug.

"Your daddy is having himself a fine day. We went walking in the garden this morning, and do you know that man ate every last bit of his lunch? Even asked for more cornbread."

"That's so good," I say, genuinely pleased. "How are you settling in here?"

After caring for Daddy at our house for so long, it was a blessing when Golden Rays offered Jessie a position when we moved him. She's able to spend time with him every day, providing a familiar face in his increasingly confusing world. It has meant so much to me and made his transition easier.

"I am loving every minute," she says, her hand near her heart. "I get to see my Bernard every day. I'm doing so much moving around, keeping these folks busy."

"I'm so glad about that." I peek past her into the room. "Is he up?"

"He naps a little after lunch, but he should be waking up soon. Go on in. Lord have mercy, he'll be happy to see his Noodle." She squeezes my arm with her large, warm hand. "Tell him I'll stop back by. Got to make sure he takes his evening medication or he'll be up all night wandering."

I enter the room quietly. Daddy is in his adjustable bed, the head slightly raised, eyes closed. The room is comfortable, decorated like his bedroom at home with familiar items— photographs on the walls, his favorite quilt at the foot of the bed, a clock radio on the nightstand tuned to WCLK, a jazz station he likes.

I settle into the armchair beside the bed and open a book I've been reading off and on, content to wait for him to wake naturally. After a few minutes, his eyes flutter open, unfocused at first, then slowly scan the room until they land on me.

"Hey," he says, his voice raspy from sleep.

"Hi, Daddy." I smile, leaning forward. I close the book and slip it into my purse.

He studies me for a moment, his brow furrowing slightly. "I know you...don't remember..."

The comment no longer stings like it once did. "Renee. I'm your daughter."

"Mmmmm." He hums like he's trying to remember that he has a daughter. "You come here before?"

"Yes, Daddy. I come see you every week."

He grunts, though I can tell he isn't quite connecting the information. "Jessie here?"

"She just left. She said you had a nice walk this morning."

"In the garden." He smiles, which does so much for his thin face.

"That sounds nice, Daddy."

His eyes drift to the early spring scene outside the window. The bushes are budding and the sun is bright. "What month is it?"

"It's March, Daddy."

"Not fall?"

"No, sir. Spring."

"Lorraine likes fall."

My heart squeezes at the mention of my mother's name. Autumn was indeed her favorite season. "Yes, she did."

His eyes seem to float about the room until they land on me again. "Lorraine coming today?"

I inhale a deep, fortifying breath. I hate having to remind my father that his wife died. "No, Daddy. Lorraine passed away, some ten years ago now."

His eyes widen, the usual panic settling in them. "My wife died?"

"Yes, sir."

He looks down at his hands, the confusion evident on his face. "I think...I knew that. I just forgot."

"It's okay. Would you like to sit up? I found a photo album in the garage." I pull the old, weathered case from my bag. It's cracked and peeling, it's so old. "We could look at some pictures."

"Pictures. Yes, good."

I press the button to raise his bed further, then help him swing his legs over the side. He's so thin, thinner than he was six months ago. The staff at Golden Rays make sure he eats regularly and moves daily, but muscle wasting and loss of bulk are part of the disease.

I sit beside him on the bed, opening the album across our laps. The first photo is of my parents soon after they met. He'd been driving back and forth from Atlanta to Memphis to see her. They were young, beaming, full of hope for the future.

"Lorraine," he says, his finger tracing the outline of my mother's face. Mine was a near carbon copy, which was why, in the early days of his diagnosis, he called me Lorraine. "So pretty."

"Yes, she was a beautiful woman."

"That's me?" He sounds surprised, staring at the black and white image. "Don't look like me."

"Well, you were younger."

"Had more hair." A glimmer of his usual caustic humor shines through, though it fades quickly.

We turn the pages slowly. Each photo prompts a different

reaction—sometimes recognition, sometimes confusion, sometimes nothing at all. When we reach a photo of me as a little girl, sitting on my mother's lap with a book, he pauses.

"Lorraine. And..." He taps the photo. And looks at me.

"And me. I was a little girl."

"Reading a book."

"Yes," I say. "Mama loved books. She opened a bookstore. You ran it for a long while when she died. Gladwell Books. Do you remember the bookstore Daddy?"

He doesn't hear me. Or doesn't want to answer. He stares at the photo, his eyes narrowing slightly as if trying to piece together fragments of memory.

"Your mama...read books to you."

This moment of recall, fragmented though it is, catches me off guard. I smile, surprised he made the connection. "She did. Every night."

We continue through the album. Pictures of family vacations, school events, holidays. My high school graduation. Each image is a piece of our shared history, though most of it is lost to him now.

When we reach the end, I close the album and set it aside.

"Would you like some water, Daddy?"

He nods, so I pour him a glass from the pitcher on his nightstand and place a straw in the glass. He drinks slowly, water dribbling down his chin. I pluck a tissue from the box at his bedside and gently wipe it away with a tissue.

His eyes light on my face suddenly, with an intensity that surprises me.

"You're sad," he says.

The observation catches me off guard. I set the glass of water on the nightstand. "I'm sad?"

"The man?"

The question comes unexpectedly, almost as if from the old

Bernard, the father who would pester me to open up about whatever was bothering me.

"Uh....the man..."

I smile. He's trying to remember Malcolm's name. They became the best of friends when he moved in.

"How did you know I was thinking about Malcolm?"

Daddy shrugs, his eyes drifting back to the window. "I know." His words come slowly, deliberately. "Where... is...the man?"

I laugh softly. "Malcolm is at work."

"He... good?"

"Yeah, he's fine Daddy. I will tell him you asked about him."

After a moment, he looks at me again. "He's good...to you?"

I'm beginning to tear up. Not this man with a shred of memory trying to make sure the man I picked treats me well. It occurs to me that while he was indifferent to my ex-fiancé, Marcus, he never got the chance to approve or disapprove of Malcolm.

"Yes, Daddy. He is very good to me."

"Mmmmm." He seems satisfied. "That's nice."

His gaze returns to the window, his attention shifting. Then, almost as an afterthought, he murmurs, "Noodle."

The nickname—one he hasn't used in a while—makes my breath catch. "What did you say?"

"Hmm."

"You called me Noodle. That's what you used to call me when I was little."

His expression is blank now. The moment of clarity was fleeting. He has already lost the thought.

I sit with him in silence for a while longer, holding his hand. It is bony and his hand doesn't close around mine. It doesn't matter if he consciously remembers or if those brief words were random firings in his deteriorating brain. For a few moments, some part of him recognized me—not only as a familiar face, but as his daughter. It's more than I've had in months.

"I should go, Daddy," I say after a while. "Jessie will come back to help you with dinner and your meds."

He begins to get up. "Dinner time already?"

"Almost," I tell him, pulling him back down. "I'll come see you again next week, okay?"

"Okay." He squeezes my hand weakly. "Noodle."

If I don't get out of this room, I will burst into tears. I'm so touched that he's retained this small piece of information, even if it might be gone again soon. I lean in and kiss his forehead.

"I love you, Daddy."

He pats my hand. "Good girl. Like your mama."

It isn't "I love you too." But in his own way, it's just as meaningful.

I sit in my car and process, like I always have to do after a visit with my father.

The nickname. The observation about my eyes looking sad. His question about *the man* and if I was being treated well. Maybe it was a random collection of moments where the fog lifted slightly.

Or maybe it was a sign that somewhere deep inside, my father is still there, still looking out for me in his own way.

When I get home, the house is empty. Malcolm texted that a last-minute client issue came up and he'd be late. I heat up leftovers for dinner and eat alone at the kitchen table, scrolling through catalogs to decide which books to order.

Lexie sent over a draft plan for the book club, complete with reading lists, activity ideas, and a proposed budget. I make a few notes and send it back with my approval. We'll need to order new titles, but the potential to bring in a whole new group of readers is worth the investment.

After dinner, I clean up and decide to take a long bath. The hot water and lavender bath salts help ease some of the tension I've been carrying all day, but my mind is still heavily occupied by something that should not take up so much rent free space.

By the time I hear the garage door roll open, I'm in my pajamas, curled up in bed with the latest Kennedy Ryan release I took from this week's UPS delivery.

Malcolm appears in the doorway a few minutes later, his tie already loosened and his jacket tossed over one arm. He looks exhausted, but his eyes glow when he sees me.

"Hey, babe," he pushes out with a sigh. "Still up? It's late for you."

I insert my bookmark and set the book aside. "You had a long one."

"The longest." He begins undressing, hanging his suit carefully in the closet. "This new client Brent signed on is a pain in my ass. You can't change the entire security protocol less than a week before a public event. It affects staffing, I have to make sure we have coverage at every entry and exit point. We had to rebuild everything from scratch."

"Oh, that's not stressful."

"Not at all."

He disappears into the bathroom, and I hear the water running as he washes his face and brushes his teeth. When he emerges, he's wearing only boxer briefs, most of his fit body on full display. Despite everything on my mind, I appreciate the view.

Malcolm slides into bed beside me. I giggle when he immediately pulls me to his side of the bed and into his arms. When he is comfortable, he inhales a deep breath and blows it out.

"Missed you. Didn't have a chance to text you or anything."

I grin. "I missed you too."

"You see your dad today?"

I snuggle even closer, resting my head on his chest. "Yep. He called me Noodle."

Malcolm's hand, which had been stroking my back, pauses. "Really? He hasn't done that in—"

"Forever. Yeah." I tilt my head up to look at him. "He knew I was his daughter. He asked if I was sad, then asked if about *the man*."

Malcolm chuckles. "Oh, no. You got my man Bernard mad at me?"

"No. I think he wanted to tell me to not worry."

"Smart."

"But demented...so..." I trace patterns on his chest with my fingertip. "I've been overthinking about tomorrow."

Malcolm catches my hand in his, brings it to his lips. "I meant what I said last night. It's strictly business."

"I know. It's not even about Charlene. Not really."

"What is it really about?"

I hesitate, searching for the right words. "The other night, you said you dodged a bullet when you divorced her. And that you weren't going down the marriage road again. And...I—" I can't finish the sentence for some reason.

Malcolm is quiet for a long moment. Then exhales. "I knew that comment was gonna bite me in my ass."

"It's not about the comment. It's about what's underneath it."

He shifts, propping himself up on one elbow to look at me properly. "I wasn't talking about you, Renee. About us. I was talking specifically about my disaster of a marriage to that particular woman."

"I know, but—"

"No, no. Let me clear this up." His eyes are serious, intense. "When I said I wasn't going down that road again, I meant I wasn't going to let myself be manipulated, controlled, or betrayed like that again. By that woman. It wasn't a blanket statement about marriage."

I bite my lip.

"Is that what's been bothering you? You thought I was saying I'd never get married again, period?"

"Kind of. Well...yes."

"Okay. Well, I'm saying that doesn't apply to me and you. I was kind of waiting to get the high sign that you wanted to head in that direction."

"Consider the flag thrown on that. And... other things."

Malcolm laughs at my cryptic hinting. "What other things?"

This is it. The perfect opening to tell him everything that's been on my mind. My desire for marriage, for children, for the Brooks name and a future that includes all the things I'd never thought I wanted until now.

But the words stick in my throat. As much as I've been thinking about it and yearning for it, I'm not ready to vocalize it. But I will be.

"It can wait until you get back from DC," I say instead. "You have enough on your plate right now."

Malcolm studies me for a moment. "I can walk and chew gum, Renee. If that's the way you want it, fine. But when I get back, we're having this conversation. ASAP."

"Promise?"

He kisses me then, slow and sweet at first, then deeper, more insistent. I melt into him, letting physical connection say what words can't. Malcolm's kiss is like a spark that ignites a fire. I respond eagerly, my body arching towards his as our lips move together.

"I love you, Renee," he whispers. "I'm coming home to *you*."

He rolls me onto my back, his body covering mine. His weight is comforting, grounding, his skin warm. I wrap my legs around his, pulling him closer, needing to feel all of him. Malcolm's hands are everywhere, caressing, stroking, teasing. Each touch sends shivers through my core. My nerve endings sing with the sensation.

His fingers slip between my thighs, finding me already slick with desire. I gasp into his mouth as we become one.

"Renee..."

"Malcolm..."

"I got you," he murmurs against my lips and moves inside me. "Right now. Next month. Next year. Next lifetime. Let me take care of you."

And he does. With his hands, his mouth, his body, he worships me, bringing me to the edge again and again before finally pushing me over in an explosion that leaves me trembling and boneless beneath him.

After, we lay tangled together, sweat cooling on our skin. Malcolm presses soft kisses to my shoulder, my neck, my jaw before rolling over.

When he is breathing deep and even beside me, I think about what Daddy asked, in his own way. If Malcolm was good to me.

Malcolm is right for me. I know that bone deep. And after tonight, I feel more confident that we want the same things.

I just have to be brave enough to ask for them. When Malcolm has put the last dredges of his old life to rest, we will move forward. With everything.

No more holding back. No more waiting for signs. I'm ready to create our future together.

eight

DEBRA

"I still can't believe you got that giant cup," Willard says as we walk across the expansive Lowe's parking lot. The mid-morning sun beams heat across the asphalt, hinting at the day's potential. "It looks like you're drinking a gallon of coffee."

I sip from my venti iced latte, savoring the dark roast. "And I will drink every last drop. I need this caffeine if we're making furniture decisions."

"We're just looking," Willard reminds me, the accountant in him already asserting itself. "Gathering information. Comparing options."

"Which is code for we'll be here until closing while you calculate the cost-benefit ratio of each option," I tease.

Willard's mouth quirks into the half-smile I've loved since we were teenagers. "I recall spending forty-five minutes deciding on a shade of blue for the guest bathroom."

"That was different," I counter. "Cerulean and azure create

completely different impacts. A bathroom color should be soothing."

"If you say so, dear."

The automatic doors slide open, welcoming us into the cavernous store. Shoppers mill about with carts filled with supplies to knock off weekend warrior to-do lists.

"I printed out the store map," Willard says, pulling a folded paper from his pocket. Because of course he did. "Home office displays should be straightforward, then to the right."

We navigate through kitchen and appliance aisles, occasionally stopping to examine something that catches our eye.

"What time did Kendra leave the house this morning?" Willard asks. She'd popped into the bathroom while he was in the shower to shout her morning salutations before leaving with her friends.

"Early," I answer with a grunt. She can be up and out the door at 6:30 on a Saturday for Robotics team, but I can't drag her out of bed during the week for school. "Today is their last full day before competition next week. She said they had a lot to get done."

"What time is that? I want to make sure it's on my calendar."

"It's on your calendar," I reply, pausing to look at a display of pendant lights. "Next Wednesday. Opening ceremony at four. Her team competes at seven-thirty."

Willard checks his watch—a habit so ingrained I doubt he realizes he's doing it. "That's all she can talk about lately. I'll be happy to go back to talking about who is cute in whatever K-pop group she is obsessed with."

"She gets that from you, you know. Laser focus."

"The perfectionism, maybe," Willard concedes. "I am no engineer. She gets to talking about mechanical stuff and..." He shrugs.

I smile at the pride in his voice. "She mentioned the navigation component was giving them trouble?"

"If it's not a number divisible by another number or classified in the tax code, I don't know. She lost me after the first five minutes of explanation."

"I like how you pretend to get it."

"Mmmph," he grunts. "Beats pretending to understand Korean pop music."

We reach the home office section, where several mock setups display various configurations of desks, shelving, and storage solutions. Willard immediately gravitates toward a large L-shaped desk with clean lines and ample surface area.

"This one has potential," he says, his fingertips dancing along the surface. "I don't know if it'll fit..."

Of course, he pulls a tape measure from his pocket. I watch him measure, then take out his phone to snap pictures of the price tag and item number.

"Isn't it premature to be investing in expensive office furniture?" I ask carefully. "Given what I accidentally overheard the other night?"

Willard's hand pauses mid-motion. "What did you accidentally overhear?"

"Your call with Barry. About wanting you back in the office full-time."

He sighs, putting his phone away. "Yeah. I was going to bring that up this weekend."

"It's the weekend." I sip more coffee and train my eyes on his.

Willard moves to a nearby office chair, testing its support as he spins from right to left and back again. "Barry called an all-hands meeting for next Friday. Attendance mandatory, no remote options. I think it's their way of signaling the end of flexible arrangements, especially during tax time."

"But your numbers are fine, right?"

"It's never about the numbers, Debra. It's about control and maintaining status quo. The way things have always been done."

"I know what status quo means." I lean against a display desk. "So...I ask again, why are we shopping for home office furniture if they're forcing you back?"

Willard's eyes don't meet mine. He kicks a sneakered foot out, setting the chair in a violent spin before it stops again. "Maybe..." he finally says, "I don't plan to stay at Willoughby."

I'd suspected this was coming but hearing him say it aloud excites me. "You're finally moving to start your own firm."

"Thinking about it." He stands, moving to a bookshelf display, running his fingers along the shelves.

"Willard, we're in the middle of Lowe's looking at mock office set ups. You're past thinking about it."

"Okay, I'm seriously thinking about it. I've been talking to some of my individual clients. Testing the waters."

"And?" I hike a brow, encouraging his response.

"Eight have already said they'd follow me. Three more could possibly follow. That's enough to start with, if I ramp down to part time. Willoughby has too much work to fire me and they can only hold partnership over my head if I don't toe the line and return to office. At this point, I don't give a damn about my name being on that masthead. I'll create my own masthead."

The way I want to shout and wave my hands like we're in a fiery Pentecostal church service... instead, I sip my now watery coffee and watch in awe of the precision with which he examines each piece of furniture.

"So...why haven't you pulled the trigger? You've been talking about this for years."

"You know why," he says simply.

And I do. Because Willard is responsible. Because he's always been the stable one, the provider. Because after everything that happened with Morningside, after I lost my job and had to rebuild my career from scratch, he wouldn't risk our family's financial security.

"I don't know if now the right time but they might be forcing my hand."

"What if I told you something that could change the timeline?" I move closer, lowering my voice though no one is nearby. "Ms. Henry called me into her office on Tuesday. She's retiring at the end of the year."

His attention sharpens. "And?"

"And...she wants me to apply to replace her as Director of East Lake Community Center."

Willard's expression gives nothing away, but I see him mentally calculating, assessing, analyzing. "Tell me more."

I explain what the job would entail—overseeing all youth and community programs, managing budgets, developing new initiatives. So much like my job at Morningside without the educational system bureaucracy.

"It would mean less direct time with the kids, more administrative work. But the impact could be greater, more far-reaching across all programs."

"The salary? Benefits?"

"Competitive. Not what I made as principal, but better than I'm bringing home now. Full benefits. Nice retirement package."

I can practically see the spreadsheets forming in Willard's mind as he processes this information.

"Willard, if I get this job, you could transition to your own practice without risking our financial security. I could be the safety net while you build your client base. The timing couldn't be better, and it's exactly what we need. What I need. I've been hiding out at ELCC, doing work I'd stopped doing as I moved up the ranks to principal."

A couple wanders into the area we've been sitting in. We take it as a sign and get up to move through more displays, examining different office configurations. Willard takes notes on his phone, documenting the options that might work best.

"I kind of like the first one we looked at," I comment. "It's a nice light wood so it doesn't make the room seem small. You need to figure out if it would fit in there."

"I'm sure it comes in pieces. We can get it in there. I don't know if I like light wood though. I like a dark walnut."

"We could keep looking around. You need to decide what you want it to look like. Maybe Kendra can find you one of those online programs to mock up the room?"

"That's a good idea. So..." He tips his head toward the next aisle. "You think you want an administrative role again? Morningside about did you in. About did us in."

The question hits exactly where I'm most vulnerable. We both know what happened the last time I was in a position of authority. The way I nearly destroyed everything we'd built together and how it rippled out in waves through everyone connected to us. Including our daughter. My scandal was the biggest reason we'd moved Kendra to a new school.

"I'm ready to lead again so long as I don't lose connection with the kids. I'm not the same person I was," I say quietly. "Neither of us is."

"No," Willard agrees. "We're not."

"I don't want to go backward, Willard. I don't want you to feel like you have to go back to eighteen-hour days in the office, away from me and Kendra so we can have health insurance. And truthfully, we don't have to stay in the house. If we need to downsize, my best friends would love for us to move closer to my job."

Willard pauses at a walnut desk with built-in shelving. "I like this one a lot," he says, seemingly changing the subject. But I know he's processing, thinking through everything I've said.

"It looks like the first one you saw, but it's the dark wood you like."

"What does Ms. Henry say about your chances?"

"She wants to champion me to the board. She thinks my experience at the center and my administrative background make me a strong candidate."

"Okay. Sounds like it might be a go. What do you have to do now?"

"Meet with Theodore West." I smirk. "You remember him from city council meetings back in the day?"

I note a roll of his eyes. Dr. West is not easy to forget. He is set in his ways and is considered 'old school.' Despite advancing Ms. Henry to the highest position at the community center, he hadn't previously been a fan of women in leadership roles.

"Yeah, I remember Theodore," he says, his tone neutral but I detect a hint of wariness. "How is he involved?"

"He is the advisory board liaison with the city. They need his approval to hire someone to replace Eleanor."

Willard takes another picture of the desk setup, this time from a different angle. "You worried?"

"I'm nervous," I admit. "About the politics, the scrutiny. I can't run from it anymore, though. If it's not this role, it could be something else months from now. How long should I be expected to hide? I know who I am now and what I want."

We continue examining furniture, discussing the merits and variety of storage solutions and ergonomic features. It feels good, this normal Saturday morning activity with my husband. This ability to move between meaningful conversation and mundane decisions.

"I think we should hold off on purchasing anything," Willard says finally. "Check a few more stores, decide on a cohesive design approach."

"Always the methodical one," I say with a smile.

"Don't think I didn't notice your little comment about moving back to the south side of town, right after we enrolled Kendra in a school near our current home."

A giggle escapes. "It's not a serious proposal, Willard."

Then I pause, letting the idea roll around in my brain. Renee had suggested it at drinks the other night and I immediately let it slide out of my consciousness, but now... it doesn't sound like a bad idea. Kendra would be out of high school in three years, off to college somewhere, but hopefully within driving distance of us. We didn't need a large, sprawling home near Morningside Middle School anymore.

"I see the wheels turning, while you're saying it's not a serious proposal."

We head back to the car. My phone chimes in my pocket with a notification. I pull it out, expecting a promotional message from one of the many retail lists I need to unsubscribe from. But it isn't.

"Oh, shit," I say, scanning the message. My pulse quickens and I blink quickly to clear my eyes, ensuring I read what I thought I read. "Dr. West wants to meet with me and Ms. Henry. Monday at eleven."

Willard waits, watching my expression and reaction.

"Oh, this is happening fast," I say, my voice tight. "He doesn't even have my application package yet."

"So what does it mean, to meet right now?"

"No idea. Maybe he wants to talk about..." My voice trails off. I'm suddenly so nervous I can't even think.

"Your past doesn't define you, Debra," Willard says, unlocking the car with a beep.

"I'll tell Dr. West that when he rolls out my rap sheet showing that I was forced to resign from my last administrative position."

"You weren't forced to resign," Willard reminds me, pausing at the passenger side door. "You've been at East Lake two years now. They've seen your work. They've taken advantage of your dedication. Ms. Henry wouldn't put your name forward if she didn't believe in you."

"What if it's not enough?"

"You won't know unless you try," Willard says simply, opening my door. "This is attempt number one. Might be the last one. Might not."

I get in the car, waiting for Willard to walk around to the driver's side. He gets in, then closes his car door and rolls down the window.

"I'm starving after all that indecision. Lunch?"

"Yes, please. Something substantial."

"I could go for a Ruby's fried chicken plate right about now."

"Perfect," I agree, pulling the seatbelt across my lap and securing it with a resounding click.

"I'm getting a slice of pie to take home," Willard adds. After years of my health-conscious meal planning, his frequent cravings for sweets have become something of a running joke between us.

Willard starts the car and pulls out of the parking space. As we drive toward Ruby's, I'm working hard to calm the preliminary nervousness and anticipation swirling in my stomach.

"It's just a meeting," I remind myself quietly. Then repeat it over and over.

"Just a meeting," Willard repeats with me. His hand rests

atop the steering wheel of his Lexus. "Got a good feeling about this meeting though. Could mean a lot of changes."

We drive toward Ruby's, the familiar route taking us past landmarks of our shared history. As we stop at a red light, Willard reaches over and briefly squeezes my hand, a small gesture that speaks volumes.

nine

MAXINE

Virgil and I decide to take a mid-morning field trip to survey a series of vacant commercial spaces. I want to get a sense of the inventory and picture the potential. I'm seeing great potential so far.

High ceilings with exposed beams. Polished concrete floors. Raw brick walls telling stories of a building's industrial past.

"This could work for a high-end boutique," I say, my heels clicking against the floor as I pace the perimeter.

"Mmmmm. I think there are too many hard surfaces for a clothing boutique but maybe something for the home?"

"A luxury eyewear brand, perhaps."

Virgil pivots in his loafers, the arm of his sporty shades in his mouth. "The location is prime. Walking distance to the major shopping districts, but far enough off the main drag to feel exclusive."

"Like you're in on a secret." I run my hand along the exposed brick. "What's the asking price?"

He consults his tablet. "The owner is looking for $2.1 million. It's been on the market for months, though—"

"Which means we could get them down to $1.5." I muse, running numbers in my head. "This area is up and coming but it's not yet worth spending over a million, a million-and-a-half. And the building needs some work."

"Agree. And your rule is that you don't do foreclosures and fixer-uppers."

"True. I think that rule has to relax a bit for commercial."

Virgil makes a note. "I've got three more properties to show you today. All with similar potential."

My phone rings in my hand. Joseph. Again. I push out an impatient huff, silence it and go back to the notes I'm typing so I can remember them later.

"Everything okay?" Virgil asks, one perfectly groomed eyebrow hiked high.

"Fine." I wave away his concern. "Joseph is working my nerves lately. Let's get moving. I want to see everything before I pick up Imani from my mother's."

We spend the next few hours viewing properties, each one reinforcing my vision for Donovan's expansion into commercial real estate. In the back of my mind, burrowing deep are the retorts I keep thinking to the argument Joseph and I had this morning.

The same one we've been having for weeks with increasing volume and intensity.

"I told you I was in the running for a promotion," he said, launching a missile from his sink in our bathroom.

I turned to him, my toothbrush halfway to my mouth. "You did? When?"

"A few weeks ago." He spit into the sink, rinsed his mouth.

"You don't remember? Senior VP of Investment Strategy. Corner office, bigger bonus structure, direct line to the Managing Director."

I honestly don't remember him mentioning a promotion, but my attention has been so divided and I've admittedly only given him slivers. "So is it a done deal?"

"Pretty much. I got the high sign from my boss last night."

"Okay. So what does that do to your schedule? You work from home part time right now to be here with Imani."

Joseph's face clouded over. He wiped his mouth on a hand towel and turned to face me, leaning against the vanity. "They want me in the office full-time. And..." He'd paused, studying my reaction. "There will be some travel involved. Quarterly trips to New York, monthly visits to regional offices."

"Okay. I guess that's expected. You're leadership. You should be in the office."

"So it means Imani will spend more time with your mother."

"You say that like it's a bad thing. She takes great care of her granddaughter. So does your mom, when she has her."

"Maybe it's time to look into a nanny. Or...maybe it's time for you to take my suggestion to pull back at Donovan. I want Imani to be raised by her parents, not—"

I huffed, planting a fist on my hip. "By *her parents* you mean *me*. I notice how you have excused yourself from that definition when you are the one going back to the office full time."

Joseph took a deep breath, clearly trying to keep his cool. "All I'm saying is that we need to reevaluate our priorities as a family. I'll be able to provide more than enough for us financially. You don't need to keep up a breakneck pace."

I bristled at his words. "I don't keep up a breakneck pace. Real estate is...like this. A lot, especially in the spring. I should give up the company I started because you got a promotion?

Donovan Realty is my business, Joseph. I've poured my heart and soul into building it from the ground up."

He rolled his eyes. "You know that's not what I meant."

"Really? Because it sounds exactly like what you said a few weeks ago, when you told me I should consider paring down my business commitments now that we have a family."

From a few rooms away, the wails of an unhappy baby cut through the tension. Joseph sighed, beginning to turn away from the sink.

I tossed my toothbrush to the counter and sighed. "I'll get her. You get dressed for work."

After the final property viewing, I save my notes, wave goodbye to Virgil and finally brave my messages. Three missed calls and a text:

> JXG: Let's talk things through. We can both have what we want. love u.

I need my mother's perspective before I face him. Inell always knows how to cut through my drama and get to the heart of things. Besides, I need to pick up Imani.

Forty-five minutes later, I pull into the driveway of the house I bought for her when Donovan took off, the house that got us both out of our old neighborhood and our old life. I find her in the living room, Imani asleep in her playpen while Inell reclines on the couch in a glorious floral caftan watching Judge Joe Brown. She loves that man and cackles at him calling everyone a crackhead.

Ironic, considering she had her own battle to fight back in the day.

"You're early. She's not even up from her nap, yet," she says, muting the TV. "What's Joseph done now?"

I scowl, dropping my purse to the couch, then sitting next

to it, making myself comfortable. We never interrupt Imani's nap time. She's so cranky when she hasn't slept enough.

"Why do you assume Joseph did something?"

She fixes me with that stare of hers. "Because I know my daughter. And that's your *my man is getting on my last nerve* face."

"He got promoted," I tell her.

"Congrats to him. That's good news, isn't it?"

"On the surface, yes. It means he's moving up, making more money, more stock options, more opportunity. It also means more office time. Some travel. Less flexibility with the baby." I glance at Imani, sleeping peacefully. "He's been suggesting that I pull back at Donovan since Imani was born. He says he wants Imani raised by her parents. Right when he is about to go back to full time office work."

"Mmmmm." Inell shifts, sitting up. "And you're about to expand the business."

"Which is a plan he is not really on board with. I can't give up my dreams because his work schedule changes," I tell her, letting the frustration seep out. "That's not fair."

Inell pauses for a moment, considering her words carefully. "Max..."

"You are not about to take up for him. I know you're not."

"Excuse me, young lady," she says, rearing back at my outburst.

No matter how good a relationship I had with Inell, I was never one to assert myself aggressively with her. She commanded respect.

"Now, you know I'm always on your side," she continued, "And I'm proud of everything you've built with Donovan Realty. But marriage is about compromise and finding a balance that works for both partners."

"He's not compromising anything. Why should I have to compromise?"

"What was your reaction to his promotion?"

The question catches me off guard. "I... asked what his new job meant for his schedule."

"Mmmhmmm," she hums. "See, you're both trying to grow and figure things out as you go. The question is, are you growing together or growing apart? You've got to get this handled, Maxine, or you're going to lose a very good man."

"Obviously, I don't know how to be the wife and mother he wants and the businesswoman I am," I admit.

"Child, listen to me," says Inell. "I raised you alone, doing what I had to do to keep you fed and in clothes that fit. You saw me at my lowest, but you also saw me survive."

She gestures around the room. "You bought me this house. Got us out of that neighborhood. Did it all legal and proper. Now you've got a man who loves you, a beautiful baby, and a thriving business. The problem isn't the promotion or the schedules or even the business. The problem is you're both so busy protecting your individual positions that you've forgotten you're on the same team. Come at it from that angle. And honey, you both might have to compromise some."

Imani stirs in her playpen, making little sounds that signal she's about to wake up. I move to pick her up before she can cry.

"The difference between you and Joseph," Inell continues, watching me settle my daughter against my shoulder, "is that you grew up having to fight for everything. He didn't. He probably had things pretty easy, in comparison. When he suggests changes, you hear threats. And when you push back, he hears rejection."

I let my mother's words sink in as I rock Imani gently. She's right, of course. Joseph and I come from different worlds. It's part of what drew us together, the way his stability and support balanced my drive and ambition.

"So now you know every fuckin' thing?" I joke. "Since you got your degree and everything?"

"Do not curse in my grand-baby's ear, Maxine."

I look down at Imani, her little face so peaceful as she drifts in and out of sleep and feel a pang of guilt.

"And I've always been wise. You have to be ready to hear it. These days, your ears can hear my wisdom."

The house is quiet except for faint sounds from Joseph's office. Imani is awake and usually post nap she is content to play with her toys while I make dinner. I settle her in her Pack 'n Play and follow the sound of Joseph's voice, pausing in the doorway. He's in front of his computer, jacket off, sleeves rolled up. By the sounds of it, he's wrapping up a call.

He notices me and signs off quickly.

"Hey," he says, pushing his chair back, then swiveling to face me.

"Hi."

"We gotta talk, baby. Like, real talk."

"Yeah." I move into the office, perching on the edge of his desk. "We do."

"I've been thinking—"

"Joseph, can I—"

I cross my arms, uncross them. I am uncomfortable being this person, and I can only be this person when I have to be this person.

"First, I apologize. I don't want to be a wife who holds her husband back and doesn't celebrate his accomplishments. This promotion is huge for you. You have worked hard for it, and I'm honestly so very proud of you. I love you with all my heart. That is what I should have said this morning."

"Thank you. Truly. I love you more." He studies me carefully. "Sounds like there is an addendum to your statement coming."

"Because there is. I need you to understand that Donovan isn't a nine to five gig. It's not a part time job where I can cut my hours. It's who I am. It has my name on it. It's the bridge between who I was and who Inell was to who we are now. I can't walk away from it any more than you could walk away from your job."

Joseph is quiet for a long moment. Then he says, "I don't want you to walk away from anything. I just worry about trying to do it all and if anything has to go so we can have a family, it's these damn jobs. You're right though; both of us have demanding careers, a baby, a house..."

"We are also both brilliant people. We will figure it out," I say, echoing my mother's wisdom. "As partners. We are on the same team, honey."

"Okay. So what does *figure it out* look like?"

"It looks like me supporting your promotion and the travel it requires. And you supporting the work I do, while making it clear to your bosses, just like I make it clear to my staff, that your family is a priority."

I hear Imani starting to fuss in the other room. When she quiets down, I continue.

"Maybe we do need a nanny to fill in the blanks, but not so I can quit working and be here to serve you martinis when you walk in the door and be Suzy Homemaker. That's never been me. That's never going to be me. What *is* me is making this work so we can both pursue our goals while knowing our daughter is well cared for."

"And the in-office requirements?"

"We adjust to whatever your schedule looks like since it's more rigid. Maybe I take more afternoon meetings so I can be home in the morning. Maybe we alternate who does drop-off and pickup, who goes in late and leaves early—the point is to figure it out together instead of trying to force me into a box labeled primary parent. I distinctly remember us both enthusiastically making her. She is both of ours."

Joseph smiles at the memory of the exact night we conceived Imani. Then he stands and moves closer, taking my hands in his. He brings them to his lips, then rolls his eyes up to mine.

"Maxine," he says, his tone a low, seductive rumble. At this moment, I know this fight is over.

"Joseph," I reply, trying and failing to match his tone.

He exhales a breath through his nose, then asks, "When did you become a reasonable person?"

I laugh. "Don't get used to it." But I'm smiling as I squeeze his fingers. "I had a talk with my mother."

"Ah." He nods deeply. "That explains it."

"Explains what?"

"You always start to make sense after a conversation with Inell."

I suck my teeth. "Whatever. You're her favorite and she always takes your side."

Joseph leans in and presses those gorgeous lips to mine. They linger for a beat longer than usual before he pulls back.

"I love you, Maxine Elise Donovan Glass. I wish I would have known what I was getting myself into when we met...but I'm in it, now. And I don't want out."

"I love you too. And I'm stuck, too. So...here we are. Stuck together."

Imani's fussing turns into full-blown crying. It's time for dinner and her bedtime routine. His phone buzzes with an incoming call. Mine probably has dozens of emails waiting.

I'm almost ready to hop down from the desk and grab her so he can take his call, but I watch Joseph silence his phone without checking it, then leave his office to attend to his daughter's demanding screams.

ten

DEBRA

My fingers tug at my lapels, a nervous habit I've had my entire life.

The grimy staff bathroom mirror will have to suffice for my fit check, as the kids say. Navy blue shift dress in a conservative cut, black blazer, modest heel. Professional, but not trying too hard. Maxine convinced me to buy this dress when I interviewed at East Lake Community Center. It still fits well, and the color complements my complexion.

I smooth my hair, tucking a strand behind my ear. The gray at my temples stands out more today. Or maybe I'm scrutinizing myself more than usual today. I debate whether to apply lipstick but decide against it. Natural works better.

"You've got this," I tell my reflection. "You know this center inside and out. You know these kids. You've earned this shot."

My phone buzzes on the counter.

> Willard: Good luck today. You're more than qualified. Don't let West intimidate you. You got this.

I smile, type back a quick *Thank you* with a heart emoji, and take one last look in the mirror. Ten minutes until my meeting with Eleanor Henry and Theodore West.

When I walk into the main area of the center, our receptionist, Diya, is seated at the front desk. Neat box braids fall over one shoulder as she tilts her head. At twenty-four, she brings an energy to the center that the kids respond to immediately, and she maintains a professionalism beyond her years.

"Looking sharp, Ms. Debra," she says. "You got your interview fit on. Big meeting?"

"Something like that," I respond, not wanting to broadcast my potential interview for Ms. Henry's job. "How was your weekend?"

Diya smiles. "It was fun. Daniel is finally in pull-ups overnight. Three whole days of no diapers at night." She dances in her seat. "It has been glorious."

"The small victories," I say with a laugh. "Those matter."

"Truth." Her smile fades slightly as she glances at the clock. "Ms. Henry told me to send you straight in. Dr. West is already here."

My stomach tightens. Of course he is early. I inhale slowly, filling my lungs until my chest tightens, then exhale the anxiety through pursed lips. Control what you can control, I remind myself and walk down the hallway to Eleanor's office.

The door stands slightly ajar; my pulse quickens as I approach—familiar territory, this flutter of nerves before stepping into a room where my future hangs in the balance.

I knock lightly.

"Come in, Debra." Ms. Henry's voice cuts through the door, crisp and authoritative, brooking no delay.

I push open the door. Ms. Henry sits behind her desk, her gray hair in a neat bun, wearing a teal blouse that brings out her hazel eyes. Her signature red lipstick stands out against her pale complexion—a small act of defiance in a world that expects older women to fade into the background.

Dr. West sits in one of the chairs facing her, his back ramrod straight, with a distinguished salt-and-pepper mane of hair and beard that gives him an uncanny resemblance to Frederick Douglass. He wears the same stern expression I've seen in historical photographs, as if he's prepared to deliver a rousing abolitionist speech rather than interview me for a community center position.

"Dr. West, good to see you again. It's been a while," I say, extending my hand.

He stands, gives my hand a firm shake. "Mrs. Macklin. It certainly has been some time."

I settle into the chair beside his, cross my ankles and place my portfolio on my lap. I brought copies of my resume, letters of recommendation, and program statistics from the past year, though I don't know if this constitutes a formal interview or a preliminary discussion.

"Thank you both for meeting with me today," I begin, but he holds up a hand.

"Eleanor has pushed you to the top of her list for the Senior Director position, ahead of all other potential candidates. She insists you possess both the skills and vision necessary to continue her work here at East Lake."

"I appreciate her confidence in me," I say. "I've learned a great deal working under her leadership."

Dr. West's expression remains neutral. "What concerns me isn't your administrative capabilities. Your experience as principal at Morningside speaks for itself. What I question is whether the board can trust you with the public-facing aspects of this role. You'll represent East Lake to donors, city officials, and the broader community."

"That presents a valid concern," I acknowledge. "I understand the importance of public trust. What I can tell you is that I've spent the last year and a half rebuilding relationships in this community."

His stare remains fixed on me. "Let's address the elephant in the room. You were forced to resign from your position as Principal at Morningside Middle School after an inappropriate relationship with a staff member came to light. Is that correct?"

The directness of his question catches me off guard, though I should have expected it. The shame and regret always lurk below the surface, just waiting for moments like this.

"That isn't entirely accurate," I correct him. "I was not asked to resign. I took a sabbatical to center myself and reflect on my actions and decided not to return to Morningside. I take full responsibility for the inappropriate relationship, but your characterization of my departure misses the mark."

"Noted. Why should I believe you won't make similar errors and missteps here?"

Ms. Henry begins to interject, but I raise my hand slightly.

"That's a fair question," I say. "The short answer is that I am no longer that person. The longer answer is that I underwent extensive counseling, both individually and with my husband. I rebuilt my marriage. I learned to communicate honestly about my needs and frustrations instead of seeking validation in unhealthy ways."

I pause, meeting his gaze directly. "I also learned a painful lesson about leadership. When you hold a position of authority, your actions impact not only you but everyone who depends on you. At Morningside, I let down my staff and my students. I won't repeat that mistake."

Theodore studies me, his expression unreadable. "And your husband? How does he feel about you potentially taking on a new job similar to your prior role?"

"He is supportive," I reply.

"The board will have concerns, Mrs. Macklin," he says flatly. "Your reputation precedes you."

The comment stings, but I keep my expression neutral. "I understand those concerns. I can't erase my past, however I've worked hard to learn from it. My record at East Lake speaks for itself."

"Tell me about your vision for ELCC," he says, changing tack so abruptly, I have whiplash.

I open my portfolio and pull out a single sheet of paper. "I've identified three areas where I believe we can grow in the next year: expanded STEM programming, particularly for our youth; deeper community partnerships, especially with local minority owned businesses; and improved mental health resources for teens."

I hand him the page outlining these initiatives with projected costs and potential funding sources. I've worked on this for months, not specifically for this position but because I saw the need and the potential.

He scans the document, his expression softening slightly. "This is extensive. And thorough."

"Debra has already implemented several programs for our students," Eleanor adds. "She also secured donations of equipment from local tech companies for the computer lab, and of course our growing library is our pride and joy."

Dr. West glances up from the page. "Why the focus on STEM programming specifically?"

"Because we lack representation in those fields, and many

of our youth never receive encouragement to explore those interests," I explain. "Last month, I brought in three engineers from backgrounds similar to our students. You should have seen their faces when they realized people who looked like them design rockets and code software."

For the first time, his expression shows genuine interest. "My great-granddaughter shows aptitude in math. She's an eighth grader. It does pop up early, doesn't it?"

I smile. "She should drop into our program. We meet every other Tuesday after school."

He returns to his previous professional demeanor. "Listen... we all know the real issue isn't your qualifications, Mrs. Macklin. You blow every other candidate out of the water. However, the board will question whether someone with your history should serve as the public face of East Lake. Some members may not feel comfortable with your candidacy."

"I expect that. And I've faced opposition before," I reply, thinking of Charlotte Rogers and her years long crusade against me with the Morningside PTA. "I stand prepared to address those concerns directly. I won't hide from my past or make excuses. But I also won't let it define my future or limit what I can contribute to East Lake."

Ms. Henry adds, "Since Debra came on staff, our youth programs participation has increased exponentially."

"I don't deny Mrs. Macklin has done commendable work, Eleanor." He places my document on the desk and folds his hands together. "The director position comes with expectations and scrutiny that reflect on this organization. It's one thing to hire her at ELCC. It's another to bring her on staff. It's quite another to elevate her to senior leadership."

"Dr. West, I know my past will factor into the decision. All I ask is for the board to not judge me by my worst error, but by how I recovered from it and what I've accomplished since.

I'm human—I made a mistake, I learned from it. I moved forward. I think that makes me more equipped to lead, not less."

His eyes search mine, as if trying to read the truth there. The moment stretches between us, heavy with what remains unsaid.

"Fair enough." He stands, gathering his briefcase. "Submit your formal application by tomorrow. Include everything we discussed today, plus your specific plans for the center's financial sustainability. The board meets Thursday. This topic is already on the agenda and I would rather not give them time to push another candidate forward."

I stand as well, trying not to show my surprise at the invitation to proceed. "Thank you for your time," I say, extending my hand again.

He shakes it firmly. "I appreciate your candor today. People rarely acknowledge their failures so directly."

After he leaves, I resume breathing. Ms. Henry comes around her desk and gives me a pat on the shoulder. This is her version of a hug. I feel the tension at the back of my neck releasing.

"You did very well," she says. "He'll fight for you. I could tell."

"Really? I feel like I was filleted."

She chuckles, walking back around to her chair. "I've known Theodore West for over forty years. We've been in step with each other our entire careers. When something doesn't interest him, he makes it plain. He doesn't ask follow-up questions. He asked you several."

"So... I need to get my application together, then?"

"Today," Eleanor confirms. "The board will raise concerns, as Theodore said. But you've got a real shot at this, Debra."

I gather my portfolio, feeling cautiously optimistic. "I'll

have my application ready today. Would you review it before I submit?"

"I insist on it. Don't be shy on your application. And don't let me down."

As I walk back through the center, I notice a mother at the reception desk with Diya, filling out the sign-in sheet to use the computer lab. This explains why I do this work. Not for titles or advancement, but for moments like these, where I can see our direct impact on the community.

I pull out my phone and text Willard:

> Meeting went better than expected. Will tell you everything tonight.

His response comes immediately:

> Never doubted you for a second. Proud of you.

The words blur slightly as unshed tears flood my eyes. I blink them away, tuck my phone into my pocket, and head back to my office with my shoulders squared. I have so much work I've been ignoring to prepare for this meeting.

And now I have an application to write.

eleven

RENEE

I wake to the sound of the shower running and Malcolm's side of the bed empty. His body heat still lingers on the sheets. He has an early flight to DC, and despite his insistence that I sleep in, I always sense when he's not beside me.

I slip out of bed and pad to the kitchen to make coffee while he finishes getting ready. He thumps down the stairs and around the corner a few minutes later.

"What are you doing up?" he whispers, wrapping his arms around me from behind as I stand at the kitchen counter. "Go back to bed."

"I wanted to see you off." I turn in his embrace and press a kiss to his lips.

"Having you here makes this whole mess less of a headache."

"Not that I mind being your personal stress relief..."

He chuckles, catching the playful challenge in my tone.

"Hold that thought until tonight." His phone buzzes with a notification from the car service. "That's my ride."

I walk him to the door, where he turns to kiss me one more time. "I'll be back tonight. Don't overthink all day."

"Me? Overthink? Never." The joke falls flat, but he smiles anyway.

"I love you, Renee."

"I love you too, Malcolm. Now go, so you can come home."

After he leaves, I stand in the kitchen, listening to the silence. This house—once my parents' home—feels different when I'm alone in it. The walls hold decades of memories: my mother's laughter, my father's booming voice from his better days, and now the echoes of the life Malcolm and I are building.

I briefly consider going back to bed but know sleep would elude me. Instead, I take a long shower, letting the water beat down on my shoulders, wash away the anxiety that clings to me like a second skin. I wish the irrational fear that something from Malcolm's past might threaten what we've built could wash down the drain.

By eight o'clock, I'm in my office at Gladwell's, responding to emails I've been putting off. The bookstore won't open until ten, but there's always something that needs attention. By the time I receive Malcolm's text that he's landed safely in D.C., I've made significant progress through my inbox.

> Landed. Meeting at 10. Should be quick.

The morning rush at the bookstore keeps me busy enough to quiet the anxious voice in my head. Betty's Coffee & Smoothies, our in-house café, buzzes with students from nearby Perimeter College, their laptops open and headphones on as they sip lattes and tap away at keyboards. The study rooms Malcolm built last summer are all booked, and there's a steady stream of customers browsing the shelves.

I spot Lexie arranging a display near the front of the store. She looks up and urges me over to her. She's barely containing a giggle.

"This box Amistad sent is full of goodies," she says, gesturing to the boxes stacked beside her. "I was going to put this one in the window."

She hands a book to me. I groan at rapper 50Cent wearing an expensive blue wool suit in a casual pose on the cover. "Do not let Malcolm see that. He can't stand that dude ever since a concert in 2008."

"Him and JaRule. Look what else they sent," she says, bending to dig more books out of the box.

When I agreed to carry books from the Amistad imprint in the store, I didn't imagine they would send their entire back-list. Lexie pulls out several books and fans them out.

"I would put that Clotilda book and the Zora Neal Hurston in the window. And maybe that April Ryan... what does that say?"

"*Black Women Will Save the World.* Can I put her next to Steve Harvey, *Act Like a Woman, Think Like a Man*?"

I snort. "Stop playing with me Lexie." I eye the boxes and ask, "How many did they send?"

"More than we requested, for sure. We are going to end up sending some of these back."

"I'd like to see if we can sell them all," I say, making a mental note to update the store's website. "Get me a count so I can update inventory. We'll do some bundles. Maybe they will sell online."

"Here's the count." Lexie hands me the packing list from inside the box.

"Perfect. Thanks, Lex." I start to turn away but remember something. "Oh, I wanted to ask you about the book club—"

My phone vibrates in my pocket. I fish it out to find a message from Debra in our group chat.

> Met with Dr. West on Monday about the Sr. Director position. Put in my application on Tuesday. The board met yesterday. Haven't heard shit since! I'm freaking out a little. A lot. Help.

Before I can respond, another message pops up, this one from Maxine.

> Dr. West would be a fool not to put you through! He's also kind of a fool so... Does he still look like Frederick Douglass?

> Debra: I can neither confirm nor deny. (yes)

I smile, typing quickly.

> No way they go another week without telling you something. I say we plan for celebratory drinks Thursday.

Debra replies immediately:

> Yes please. Or consolation drinks.

> Maxine: Drama queen. You'll be fine. Did you wear the navy dress I told you to wear? You didn't wear those ugly Nine West flats you always wear, did you?

"Renee?" Lexie's voice pulls me back to the present. "About the book club?"

"Sorry." I tuck my phone away. "Yes, the book club. So, I was thinking we could prepare a fun welcome packet for the kids who sign up. A letter, some bookmarks, a reading journal and annotation tools. Like a little kit."

"Oooh..." Lexie's expression brightens. "I love that idea. I could design something this weekend?"

"If you have time. Nothing too elaborate—we don't want to blow the budget before we even start. And have Leo give the club a cool name."

"I'll get you his ideas next week."

My phone vibrates again, and Lexie gives me a knowing look. "Go ahead and check that. I can handle things out here."

I retreat to my office, pulling out my phone to find a text from Malcolm.

> In and out in 45 minutes. Heading to my sister's for lunch with my Dad.

Relief floods through me.

> How did she handle you being there?

> She sent a junior associate to handle everything. Typical Charlene.

I had pretty much stopped worrying about the meeting, but I toss my head back and laugh. Hard.

It strikes me that this woman who once held such power over Malcolm's life and who hurt him so deeply now couldn't even muster the courage to look him in the eye. The realization settles in my chest, not as vindication, but as confirmation that some chapters truly do close.

> Glad it went smoothly. Give the family hugs from me.

> Will do. Catching 5:50 flight. Can you pick me up?

Something inside me goes liquid and supple at the thought of seeing him. It's like he's been gone for months, but when he's back in my arms, we can move forward.

> Of course. I can't wait to see you. Love you.

> Love you too.

I set my phone down, aware that I'm grinning like a fool. The knot in my stomach that's been there since yesterday has disappeared. Malcolm handled business quickly, didn't have to see Charlene, and will be home tonight. Perfect.

The rest of the day passes in a whirl of inventory checks, chatting with customers, order processing and packing up books to ship. I keep one eye on the clock, making mental calculations about when to leave for the airport.

As I'm preparing to hand things over to my evening manager, my phone chimes with the group chat again.

> Maxine: Why are men? I'm exhausted. Joseph and I finally worked out all of our shit. We better not have another fight this year. I can't take it.

> Debra: Progress! Willard's seriously talking about leaving Willoughby. If I get this job, it could mean big things for us.

> Maxine: What?? That's huge!

> Debra: Too huge. Everything's up in the air, waiting for something to land.

Me: Malcolm is on his way back from DC.
Done deal. No drama with the ex.

Maxine: Of course not. He knows better than
to bring that mess home to you.

Debra: Are you still planning to talk to him
about...you know... everything?

Me: Yes. We had a prelim chat the other night
but I wanted Charlene out of the way. He said
we need to talk about it ASAP. Wish me luck.

Maxine: You don't need luck. Girl, stand up!

Me: Why?

Maxine: Nothing. It's something the girls say.
It means remember who you are and have
some self-respect. Or something.

Debra: You've got this. Let us know when we
can plan an embarrassing bridal shower

Maxine: And an embarrassing baby shower.
Remember when you two threatened to throw
me a shower at Wal-Mart? Payback is about
to be several bitches.

Me: You don't scare me, Max. I'm off to the
airport to pick up my man. Yay. :)

Debra: You are too cute, Renee. I am off to
listen to my daughter talk about robots all
through dinner. They won their competition
Wednesday and she's still on a high.

Maxine: My baby is visiting Grammy and
Grandpa Glass tonight. I will be having sex
with my husband so don't call me early
tomorrow, Renee.

I snort and put my phone away. I find Lexie standing in the doorway of my office.

"Heading out?" she asks.

"Yes, I need to pick Malcolm up from the airport. Are you good?"

"Of course. Everything's already set for tomorrow. Go get your man."

I drum my fingers on the steering wheel as I wait in the cell phone lot at Hartsfield-Jackson. Malcolm's text came through twenty minutes ago, letting me know they'd landed, but deplaning and navigating the world's busiest airport takes time.

When my phone rings with his call, I start the engine. "Hey, you," I answer, already pulling out of the parking space. "See you in five."

I join the line of cars circling toward the terminal, keeping an eye out for Malcolm among the throngs of travelers on the sidewalk. When I spot him—tall, broad-shouldered, distinctive walk, my heart skips.

Malcolm's face breaks into a smile when he sees me. He tosses his bag into the back seat before sliding into the passenger seat.

"Hi," he says, leaning over the console to kiss me.

"Hi, yourself." I kiss him back, probably longer than appropriate for airport pickup.

The drive home is quick, filled with easy conversation about his family and my day at the bookstore. I warm us up leftovers and we sit across from each other at the table.

Malcolm devours his plate while I pick at mine, my appetite diminished by nervousness about the conversation to come.

"You're quiet," he observes, wiping his mouth with a napkin. "Everything okay?"

"Thinking." I hesitate, then decide to save the serious talk for later. "About how glad I am that you're home."

His expression softens. "Me too. It was weird being back in DC, like I was visiting someone else's life. Traffic is still terrible."

"Did you see anyone besides your family?"

"Nah. I thought about calling some old friends, but I wanted to get back home."

My chest tightens with emotion. "I missed you. Is that silly? You were only gone for a day."

"Not silly at all." He stands, coming around to my side of the table, pulling me up and into his arms. "I missed you too."

We clean up dinner together, then settle on the couch to watch a show we've been following. Malcolm's arm drapes around my shoulders so I'm plastered up against his warm body.

Halfway through the episode, his head starts to droop, and soon he's fast asleep, his chest rising and falling with deep, even breaths.

I watch him sleep, studying the lines of his face, the subtle crease between his brows that never fully disappears, the curve of his lips that form such perfect smiles. I trace his features in my mind like a cartographer mapping territory that's both familiar and endlessly fascinating.

This man who came into my life when I was struggling with my father's illness, who pitched in without being asked, who saw me at my lowest and never flinched, has become the foundation upon which I'm building my future.

The thought of life without him seems impossible now, like trying to imagine breathing without oxygen.

I gently shake him awake. "Malcolm. Let's go to bed."

He stirs, blinking sleepily. "Sorry. Didn't mean to conk out on you."

"You've had a long day."

We make our way upstairs, going through our nightly routines in companionable silence. When we finally slide into bed, Malcolm pulls me to him, his arm curling around my waist. His fingers find mine, automatically intertwining as if our hands were designed to fit together.

"So," he murmurs, his voice thick with drowsiness. "About that conversation we postponed."

I tense slightly, surprised he remembered. After such a long day, I expected him to drift right to sleep.

"We don't have to do this tonight. You've been up almost twenty four hours."

"What's one more hour, then?" He shifts, propping himself up on his elbow. I can only see him in shadow but I know his eyes are intently focused on me. "I've been thinking about what you might want to tell me the entire flight home. I want to know what's on your mind."

"I mean..." I stop and start again. "It's just...so much has changed for me since we've been together. Things that weren't a priority before suddenly matter. Like I feel like I might be very unhappy if I don't get them."

"Like what?" His tone is low and non-confrontational, inviting me to continue.

I prop myself up on one elbow, gathering my courage. "Like...don't get me wrong, I love our life. But I want a life with you that feels permanent. I don't want to go another year without us talking about making this—" I motion between us. "Official and legal. I want a future that includes all the things I dismissed before I knew what it felt like to build something real with someone I love."

"Such as?" he asks, dragging more out of me.

"Marriage," I toss out. Testing, I guess, to see if he recoils.

"Children. A commitment in front of God and everybody. A big ass dress and a big fucking party."

The rest of the words tumble out in a rush. "Your ex-wife calls and you rush to another state to do her bidding and I know..."

I press a hand to his chest because I can feel his retort building. "I know, Malcolm. It's not about her, it's about who she was to you and what she had with you that I don't. I see Maxine with Imani, and something inside me aches so bad. I visit my father and imagine what our children would look like and whether they'll know him before he's gone completely."

Malcolm is quiet for several long moments, and my heart pounds so hard I'm sure he can hear it.

"Here's where you say *Damn, Renee. You're right. We should secure our future*," I tell him.

Without a word, he gets out of bed and walks to his briefcase tucked in its spot inside the closet. He rummages through it for a moment before turning on the bedside lamp. There's something clutched in his hand.

"I was going to wait," he says, sitting on the edge of the mattress. "Do something elaborate. But maybe simple is better."

He opens his palm to reveal a small velvet box. My breath catches.

"To be clear, I'm not proposing right now," he clarifies quickly. "But when I do, I wondered if you might like to wear this."

He opens the box to reveal a vintage ring with a modest but brilliant diamond set in white gold.

I gasp so loud and so sharp, I almost choke on my breath.

"The other reason I wanted to go up to DC and see Dad is because he was holding Mom's ring for me. He said it should go to the woman I want to spend my life with. Charlene never had this ring. I guess something inside me knew. But...when I went over there, he asked about you. I started talking about you and couldn't stop."

He pauses to chuckle. "He started laughing, then went and got the ring and said it was time, that I was about to have you out here looking silly for sticking by me and I haven't so much as mentioned marriage or a ring or anything. If you don't like the setting, we can use the stone to create something more your style."

I stare at the ring, speechless.

"Renee? Here's where you say *Damn, Malcolm, this ring is fire and I love it!*"

"I..I feel like Meghan Markle accepting a piece of Princess Diana's jewelry," I finally manage, making him laugh.

"I hope that's a good thing."

"It's a very good thing, baby." I take the box from him, examining the ring more closely. "It's beautiful, Malcolm. And I would be honored to wear your mother's diamond."

"So you accept my not-yet proposal?"

"As long as a real one is coming." I hand the box back to him. "On bended knee and everything."

"Promise." He sets the ring on the nightstand, turns off the lamp and slides under the covers, pulling me to him. I feel his heartbeat vibrating through my back.

"So...we talking kids too?"

"Yes. I want my father to meet his grandchild, if I can help it."

"I want that too," he says, his voice raw and unguarded. "My dad talked about how much he wished my mother could have met our kids. How she would have loved being a grand-mother. How he hopes he gets to meet them too."

He pauses, his hand finding mine, gripping it firmly. "I been thinking about a little girl. Curly hair like yours. Sweet little thing—I'd be completely done for, wrapped around her finger before she could even talk. Or a little dude to follow me around. Handsome face like either of his grandfathers."

The tenderness in his voice makes my breath catch. Tears prick my eyes, then cascade down my cheeks.

"There are these moments when my dad is so clear, you know? What if there could be one perfect moment when he holds our baby and knows that's his grandchild? I want that moment to exist in the world. I want to have that memory to hold onto when he's gone."

"That would be good for him," he whispers, his breath warm on my neck. "For you, too. For our child, even if it's brief. Bernard deserves that. You deserve that."

"So...you're really ready for all of that? The whole thing?"

"Who's ever ready? I want it. I didn't want to pressure you but I knew I needed that ring."

I laugh and turn so I face him. "Look at us. Both wanting the same thing and neither one saying it."

"We're saying it now." He kisses my forehead, then my cheek, my lips, where he lingers. "I love you. And I'm going to love creating the Brooks family with you."

"I love you, too." I curl into him, finally at peace with the future stretching before us. "Welcome home, Malcolm."

twelve

RENEE

Eighteen Months Later

The bell above the door jingles as I push my way into Ruby's, the heavy aromas of fried chicken, candied yams, and freshly baked cornbread wrapping me in a carby hug. Liam squirms in my arms, his little forehead scrunching up as if he's trying to get used to the noise of clattering dishes, sizzling grills, and loud chatter of a busy cafe brunch rush.

"Well, I'm glad someone showed up," Maxine calls out in mock admonishment as I slide into our usual booth, the worn leather seat creaking beneath me. She scowls, breaking the seal on a bottle of Perrier water and pouring it into a glass. "I was starting to think y'all forgot."

I shoot her a playful glare while adjusting Liam in the crook of my arm. "We've had a morning. Liam's been a bit demanding lately, haven't you, little man?" My finger traces the contour of his downy cheek. At seven weeks old, he's a carbon copy of Malcolm.

"Where is Debra?"

"Walking in now, according to her text," Max answers, putting her phone down.

The door swings open and Debra enters. "Sorry I'm late," she says, unwinding her scarf as she joins Maxine in the booth. "Kendra had what we call a Sephora disaster and mom had to course correct."

Ruby, supposedly retired but still showing up every so often to supervise her son, Richard, shuffles to our table carrying a pot of coffee in one hand and three oversized mugs dangling from the fingers of the other.

"Well, if it isn't Gladwell, Donovan, and Macklin together again," she drawls. "And I see you finally brought that baby boy around to see me, Renee."

"It's actually *Brooks*, Glass, and Macklin," I correct, extending my left hand with the wedding and engagement rings I can finally wear again. My fingers swelled so much during my surprise, almost instant pregnancy that I only wore my rings for a few months before they nearly needed cutting off.

Ruby winks as she fills our mugs. Steam rises from the dark liquid, and I breathe it in. I allow myself coffee on special occasions, and brunch with my girls qualifies.

"Couldn't keep him away from his Auntie Ruby for long," I tell her, shifting him for a better view. "Liam, meet the woman responsible for keeping your mama and aunties in line all these years."

Ruby's expression softens as she studies my son. "Well, aren't you the very image of your daddy," she says. "And I see some of your mama in those eyes. Even a little bit of Lorraine. Mmhmm...yes, indeed."

She straightens and looks at each of us. "It is wonderful to see you ladies in here again. Y'all ready to order?"

"Salmon croquettes and grits, please," Debra answers.

"I'll get your honey chicken biscuit," Maxine says. "No egg on that."

"I'll do the chicken and waffles, please," I order.

"Oh, and one of your fried chicken plates and a slice of your sweet potato pie to go," Debra adds. "Willard won't let me in the house if I come to Ruby's and don't bring him any pie."

Ruby's thin lips curve into a smile. "Coming right up. Holler if y'all need anything else." She shuffles away, her head keeping time with Al Green flowing through the speakers.

Maxine leans forward, eyes bright. "So...before we get into the heavy stuff, I have something special to announce."

Debra and I trade glances. Maxine's announcements never disappoint.

"Do tell," Debra urges, lifting her mug to her lips.

"Let's just say... you know what my favorite thing to do with my husband is..." Maxine's smile widens as her hand settles on her stomach.

"Oh, for heaven's sake... are you?!" Debra's voice rises with excitement.

"So you're going to reveal all your pregnancies at Ruby's?" I ask, thinking back to when she announced she was pregnant with Imani.

"What do you mean *all*?" Maxine narrows her eyes. "If this baby is a Joseph Xavier Glass replica, the shop will be closing."

I reach across the table to grasp Maxine's hand, careful not to disturb Liam. "Congratulations! I'm so happy for you and Joseph!"

"Thank you! It's still pretty early," she says, beaming. "We are about eight weeks along. But I wanted you two to be the first to know. Well, after Joseph and Inell and his folks, of course."

Debra squeezes Maxine's other hand. "How are you feeling? Imani put you through it. Any morning sickness this time around?"

"Not too bad yet, thank goodness. I sleep a lot. Hopefully this little one will go easy on me."

"So you both want a boy this time?" I move Liam to my shoulder as he begins to fuss.

"I mean, I'll be thrilled either way. But I know Joseph is secretly hoping for a little mini-me to throw a football around with."

We laugh together, picturing Joseph teaching a tiny version of himself the perfect spiral pass.

"Well, I for one can't wait to spoil another Glass baby rotten," Debra says.

"Hear, hear," I echo.

Ruby and another server interrupt our moment, arriving with plates piled high with steaming Southern favorites. My stomach responds instantly.

"Eat up, y'all," she instructs, placing our food down. "Calories don't count in here and don't even think about skipping dessert."

She doesn't have to tell us twice. For several minutes, only the sounds of forks against plates and occasional appreciative murmurs fill our space.

"We took Liam to see Daddy on Wednesday," I say, breaking our comfortable silence. "We went before lunch so he would be alert. I let him hold Liam for a little bit and he just stared at him for the longest time."

I pause, fighting the tightness in my throat. "He's so...disconnected now. You know? Sometimes he knows me, most times he doesn't. But I feel like he knew this was his grandson, that he was holding a piece of his legacy in his arms. It was the moment I wanted to have with him."

Maxine reaches for my hand, her grip firm. "I'm so glad you

got to have that with him, Renee. I know how much it means to you for Liam to know Bernard, even if it's for a little while."

I press my lips together in a small smile. We sit in shared silence, each lost in private thoughts until Maxine clears her throat.

"How's the new gig going, Deb? Senior Director Debra Macklin has such a nice ring to it."

"It's going pretty well. Lord, the politics of it all, though. Eleanor trained me before she stepped down, but there were some skeletons hiding around a few corners. Thought I was done with that nonsense when I left Morningside."

"Heavy is the head that wears the crown," I muse. "Or in your case, the feet that wear the sensible kitten heels."

"Or the ugly Nine West flats," Max interjects with disgust.

"Let it go, Maxine!" Debra says sputtering.

"I will let it go when you throw away those ugly shoes, Debra!"

Our laughter dissolves the previous moment's heaviness.

"Seriously, Deb," Maxine's voice turns earnest. "I'm so proud of you. You worked your ass off to get to where you are, and you deserve every bit of recognition and responsibility that comes with it."

A pleased flush spreads up Debra's neck. "Thanks, Max. That means a lot. I hope I can live up to everyone's expectations, you know? East Lake has been such a cornerstone of the community for so long. I don't want to let anyone down."

"You won't," I tell her with absolute certainty. "You were born for this and those kids are damn lucky to have you in their corner."

"I'm certainly going to try my best. And who knows, maybe one day soon I'll be sending some of our brightest stars your way, Renee. I heard Gladwell Books is starting a youth literacy program?"

"Well, Lexie's working on a new certification, so that always means a new project for the bookstore. She's been pulling the curriculum together for months, and we're set to launch next quarter. The idea is to design and provide books for reading programs, writing workshops, and mentorship opportunities for kids."

"It folds right into the reading program at ELCC," says Debra. "We're probably going to implement some of what Lexie is putting together. Very exciting."

"Oh, yes. Thrilling," says Max, her tone dry.

"About as thrilling as an hour-long lecture on the changes in the commercial real estate market," Debra retorts, "but we push through and pretend to be interested."

"Whatever, Debra," Maxine narrows her eyes playfully. "I was about to say Ms. Lorraine would be proud of the way you've grown her little store."

"I like to think so," I say quietly, feeling the ache that accompanies any mention of my mother. "And it puts the additional space we've added to use. Malcolm has been chomping at the bit to expand Gladwell and the second level is finally usable."

"Speaking of Malcolm..." Maxine's smile turns mischievous. "How's married life treating you these days? Is the honeymoon phase still going strong or has reality set in yet?"

"You don't see this baby in my arms? We have been *enjoying* each other, you hear me? Between the wedding, the pregnancy and giving birth, construction at Gladwell's...life is a whirlwind."

"A good whirlwind, right?" Asks Debra.

My thoughts turn to my husband and I am overcome with emotion. Malcolm, my rock, my partner through late night feedings, blowout diapers, the exhaustion and overwhelm of new parenthood has been by my side for every moment, showering Liam and me with unwavering attention and devotion.

"The best kind of whirlwind," I answer. "Don't get me started. I'm so deliriously happy."

Debra reaches over to stroke the tiny puffs of hair atop Liam's head. "You two make beautiful babies, that's for sure."

She straightens, her eyes gleaming. "I think we should toast."

"We should get drinks we can actually toast with," Maxine suggests.

"Like what, Max? I don't drink, you're pregnant and this one," she points at me, "is breastfeeding."

"I forgot about that." She frowns. "We're so old."

"Raise your damn mug, Max." Debra lifts her coffee. "To Lorraine, to Ruby, to Inell...to all the strong women who paved the way for us to be here today, living our dreams and building our futures."

Maxine and I join her, clinking mugs and water glasses together over the table.

"One last announcement," says Debra, setting her mug down and clasping her hands. "And don't hate me for holding out on this but...Willard and I put in an offer on a house in Decatur. If it goes through, we'll be neighbors again."

"Shut up! For real?" Maxine nearly shouts. The diners at tables around us gawk at the scene we're making but none of us care.

"Debra! Oh, God..." I can't help myself— I'm naturally emotional and the pregnancy hormones are still raging. I burst into violent tears and I feel my face burning red.

"Oh, Renee..." Debra moves to take Liam and pass him to Maxine before wrapping her arms around me. "This is becoming a habit, honey. We've got to have one brunch date or happy hour where we don't make Renee cry."

"Hear that, Liam? Your mama is soft," Maxine tells my son. The little traitor smiles back at her. "Oh, he liked that. Look Deb."

They laugh together at his response.

"Stop laughing at me!" I manage between sobs. "I'm just so happy!"

* * *

I settle Liam in his car seat, already fast asleep.

"Can we get back to our monthly brunches?" Maxine asks from her car. "I can't do another pregnancy without you two."

"Wouldn't miss it for the world," Debra confirms, adjusting her purse strap, heading toward her car. "I need adults to talk to."

"And I need to lean on you both so I can do this marriage and mama thing right. First Saturday of the month, come hell or high water."

I check Liam once more before getting into the car, his tiny face peaceful in sleep.

This beautiful boy, my little family, and the friendship of these remarkable women....this is my legacy. I'll be damned if I let anything get in the way of cherishing every moment of it.

afterword

I know, I know. About ten years ago I promised a follow-up to this story. There's no time like the present, right?

Brunch at Ruby's is my favorite of all of my books. It's where I recommend people start with my catalog and revisiting these ladies has been the highlight of the past six months.

I hope you enjoyed this brief visit with Debra, Renee and Maxine and satisfying conclusion to the Ruby's saga. I can't say you'll never see these ladies again. I can say that I have near future plans to spin off characters from the **Brunch at Ruby's** and **Dinner at Sam's** novels into stories I hope you'll love.

I hope you'll see the first of the spin-off novels this summer with **Missing Persons,** which features Yvette Young, the P.I. that Gibson hires in **Dinner at Sam's** to find Vanessa's husband.

Until then, keep reading!

Xoxo,

DL White

books by dl white

Brunch at Ruby's, a Ruby's novel

Dinner at Sam's, a Ruby's novel

Beach Thing, a Black Diamond Romance

Elysium, a Black Diamond Vacation Romance

The Pearl at Black Diamond, a Black Diamond Romance

Leslie's Curl & Dye, a Potter Lake Small Town Romance

Second Time Around, a Potter Lake Holiday Short

The Guy Next Door, a Potter Lake Small Town Romance

Home for the Holidays, A Potter Lake Holiday Novella

The Kwanzaa Brunch, a Holiday Short

A Thin Line

The Never List

Hey, Lover, a Second Chance Romance

Unexpected, a holiday short

The Festival at Evergreen Falls

Grumpy Valentine

Calculated Risk *(Coming Spring 2025)*